"You're not interested in this job," said Josh.

"I can't waste time hiring another housekeeper who won't last—someone who'll run out on us when the going gets rough."

"I won't run out on you. I promise."

"That's just it, Lily Ann. I can't imagine why a beautiful young lady like you would *want* this job."

Abruptly he lifted his hands and placed them on her shoulders. His grip was warm and hard, and Lily Ann's heart missed a beat, then began pounding wildly. She stood very still, waiting for him to touch her face. Gazing at his eyes, drowning in a smoky gray sea, she felt herself relinquishing all thought of returning home.

And for twenty-four hours a day, every day, she was going to have to be on guard against this man's charm.

Taking another unsteady breath, she said quietly, "I want the job. I'm sure of it."

Dear Reader,

This month we're proud to present our Premiere title for 1993—it's a wonderful love story called *Still Sweet on Him*, by an exciting new author, Jodi O'Donnell.

Jodi, a native of Iowa, has written a romance from the heart, set in a place much like her own hometown. This book was also the winner of the 1992 Golden Heart Award given by the Romance Writers of America for an outstanding unpublished novel. Look for Jodi's special letter to you in the front pages of *Still Sweet on Him*.

If you enjoy this book—and we hope you do!—look for Jodi's next book, *The Farmer Takes a Wife*, coming in February 1994.

Our popular FABULOUS FATHERS series continues this month with *Mad About Maggie*, by one of your favorite authors, Pepper Adams. And don't forget to visit Duncan, Oklahoma—where love can make miracles happen—as Arlene James's THIS SIDE OF HEAVEN trilogy continues with *An Old-Fashioned Love*.

Look for more great romances this month by Maris Soule, Marcy Gray and Linda Varner. This month and every month, we're dedicated to bringing you heartwarming, exciting love stories. Your comments and suggestions are important to us. Please write and tell us about the books and authors you enjoy best.

Happy reading!

Anne Canadeo
Senior Editor
Silhouette Romance

RAINBOW'S PROMISE

Marcy Gray

Silhouette
ROMANCE™
Published by Silhouette Books New York
America's Publisher of Contemporary Romance

To the One who gives us rainbows and always keeps His promises.

SILHOUETTE BOOKS
300 East 42nd St., New York, N.Y. 10017

RAINBOW'S PROMISE

Copyright © 1993 by Marcy Gray

ISBN: 0-373-08967-8

First Silhouette Books printing October 1993

Books by Marcy Gray

Silhouette Romance

So Easy to Love #704
Be My Wife #792
Rainbow's Promise #967

Silhouette Desire

A Pirate at Heart #477

MARCY GRAY

loves a good romance, especially if it makes her cry. She looks for story ideas in everyday life and finds ordinary, flawed people much more interesting than "perfect" ones. To her way of thinking, anyplace—even your own hometown—can be romantic if you let your imagination run free.

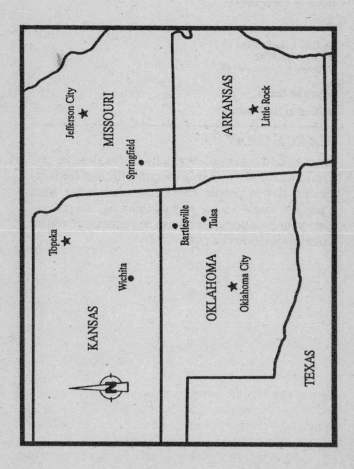

Chapter One

The man set the box on the living-room floor and gave it a nudge with the scuffed toe of his shoe. "That's all of it, kid. That's all there is left of your daddy's stuff. I been keeping it in the closet, like you asked me to do."

Lily Ann stared at the carton without moving from Homer's sofa. "Not much to show for more than fifty years of living, is it?"

Her father's oldest friend shook his gray, shaggy head. "Not a whole lot. Sorry about that, kid."

"Hey, don't apologize to me, Homer. I'm grateful you were there for Pop before he died ... and afterward, too, cleaning out his place and going through his clothes and everything the way you did. I'm glad I didn't have to handle that." Her throat tightened, and in the sudden quiet she heard Homer sniffle.

A warm spring breeze fluttered the curtains at the open window and stirred the air in the small house, sneaking under her hair and tickling the back of her neck. It made

Lily Ann laugh, and her sense of humor surfaced. "Don't you go feeling sorry for me, Homer. Not when I'm about to take possession of the family jewels!"

Homer managed to grin as he sank into his worn easy chair. They both knew that when Ned Jones died six months earlier, he'd had nothing of value to leave his only child.

The fact was, her father had never had much of anything. Never in his entire life. He had been, Lily Ann admitted with bittersweet affection, a perennial loser. Someone who only worked when he had to, and only when he wasn't drinking. Someone who probably would have drifted from place to place if he hadn't stumbled upon Wichita, Kansas, as a young man and been too contented to leave. Or too lazy.

Back when she and her father still shared the run-down apartment of her childhood and teen years, Lily Ann had often found herself wanting to shake him, to force him to take a long look at the mess he'd made of his life. He'd had little enough gumption even when her mother was alive; after her premature death, Lily Ann had felt more like the parent than Ned. She'd sworn to herself that if she had been the one in charge, she would have made sure that her family had three square meals a day and something besides other people's cast-offs to wear. But her easygoing Pop had never understood her need for order in a frighteningly disordered life, or the ironic, sometimes cutting wit with which she insulated herself. He'd never realized she held him accountable for her mother's unhappiness, either.

"Don't you want to have a look at them papers?" Homer prodded her after she'd sat lost in somber memories for a quarter of an hour. "Not that I'm rushing you. When you told me you was coming, I kinda hoped you'd stay all weekend. But you said you have to head right on back to Springfield soon as you catch your breath.''

Lily Ann didn't really have urgent business awaiting her. This was Saturday; she didn't have to be back at work at the insurance company until Monday, and her closest friends were out of town. But she couldn't bear to stay here, talking over old times with Homer. His gruff voice and two-day-old beard reminded her too poignantly of her father. He especially reminded her of the fact that she would never see Ned again. That the moment she graduated from high school she had moved to Missouri and so had been able to visit Ned only infrequently. That she hadn't been with him at the hospital when he died. Despite the differences in father and daughter—and there had been a definite chasm between them—she had loved Ned.

Maybe it was guilt driving her now, but Lily Ann couldn't wait to get away from Wichita. She almost wished that instead of tackling this long-overdue job, she'd gone camping with Kathleen and Dina.

Muffling her sigh, she slid off the couch in a graceful move, then settled down on the rug. She crossed her long, slim, jeans-clad legs Indian fashion, folded back the sleeves of her chambray shirt and drew the box closer. "Is it really necessary for me to read all this, or can I take it home and stick it on a closet shelf for another ten or twenty years?'' she asked, only half joking.

"Might want to read it,'' Homer said with an air of mystery that wasn't at all like him.

It would have been a lot less painful just to store the stuff, she thought as she sorted through the pitiful collection of items Ned Jones had saved: a matchbox full of loose pearls from the strand her mother used to wear...every report card Lily Ann had ever received...the gaudy tie tack with the American flag on it

that she had given Ned for Christmas the year she was
nine . . . the blue ribbon she'd won when she ran the fifty-
yard dash faster than any other seventh-grade girl at John
F. Kennedy Junior High School.

Lily Ann fingered the satiny award, recalling that both
her parents had watched her run that race. Later, to cele-
brate, her father had taken them out to eat hamburgers.
He hadn't been drinking, and her mother, for once, had
seemed young and free of problems.

By the time she turned back to the box, Lily Ann's
throat felt raw. Here was her parents' marriage license . . .
her own birth certificate . . . her mother's death notice,
clipped from the Wichita *Herald* ten years ago, when Lily
Ann was fourteen.

Determined not to dwell on her sorrow, Lily Ann flipped
through a stack of Ned's paycheck stubs—the history of
his irregular employment—and then picked up a bundle of
vouchers of some kind, printed on onionskin paper and
held together with a rubber band. "What's this?"

Homer shrugged. "I thought you might know."

She shook her head and sent thick blond hair whipping
back and forth across her face. Distracted, she pushed a
long strand back from her cheek. "These look like the kind
of receipts you get when you purchase a cashier's check."
She thumbed through the forms, noting that a Wichita
bank had issued them. "They're all made out to someone
named Joshua Delaney, for amounts varying from one
hundred dollars up to . . . let's see . . . two hundred and fifty
dollars." She whistled, amazed to think of her father
spending that much money on something other than rent
or food . . . or booze. "There are monthly receipts for over
four years . . . right up until the month he died. What do you
make of that, Homer?"

He had straightened up in his chair as he watched her. "You don't know who Joshua Delaney is?"

"I've never heard of him."

"Me, neither." Homer slumped again.

"Could Pop have been buying something from him?"

"Like what? I never saw Ned with anything that cost more than a couple hundred bucks—at least, not after the court took away his driver's license and he sold his car. When his TV went on the blink, he gave it to the Salvation Army. Said he couldn't afford to fix it."

"Well, if he wasn't buying anything, then why did he shell out thousands of dollars to this...this Joshua Delaney?" Her blue eyes narrowed. "Wait a sec...where's your phone book? I'm going to look him up and—"

"You won't find him in the Wichita phone book, kid," Homer interrupted her. "Joshua Delaney lives in Oklahoma. Bartlesville, Oklahoma."

"I thought you didn't know him."

"I don't, but his address is in there." He gestured to the box. "There's a stack of envelopes, all stamped and ready to go, except for being empty. It appears to me your daddy expected he'd be sending Mr. Delaney a bunch more of them cashiers' checks."

When she found the envelopes he was talking about, she focused anxiously on Homer. "Listen...you don't think...could Joshua Delaney have been blackmailing my father?"

Homer's seamed face grew glum. "That thought did occur to me. I was afraid it might have something to do with Ned losing his license. He sure didn't want folks to find out the truth about that—especially you. I was off visiting my son in California when it happened—seems like it was four years ago last fall. Guess I musta been gone six months. By the time I got home, Ned had already been to court and sold his car. He never would talk about it straight out, but one time he let it slip that he had a car wreck.''

"A wreck!" The news stunned her. "When I found out Pop's license had been suspended, I just assumed it was because he'd been caught driving while intoxicated again." She frowned, regretting that she'd only been able to see him every six months or so before he died. No telling how many other secrets he'd kept! "Why didn't he tell me, Homer?"

"Probably because you'd always warned him to quit drinking before he had an accident. Guess he didn't want you to be disappointed in him. Or mad."

Nodding, Lily Ann recalled all her dire predictions that Ned would kill himself—or somebody else—if he didn't give up the bottle. "I was so proud when he *did* quit drinking." On every visit home, she had praised Ned for staying sober, but now that she looked back on it, her praise had only seemed to depress him. She snorted. "He must've already had the accident by then. Did he keep on drinking behind my back?"

"No, he really did quit. Honest, kid."

He'd done too little, too late, she thought. "Was it a bad accident?"

Homer shrugged. "Beats me. I don't think he got hurt, but he sure was ashamed. They only took away his license for a year, but he never wanted to drive again. I think maybe Delaney must have found out about the accident somehow and Ned started paying him to keep quiet. Fact is, he made me swear on a stack of Bibles I'd never tell you. I'd say his biggest fear was that you'd get wind of it."

Unwonted sympathy stabbed Lily Ann as she pictured her ill father, hunched over as he walked the two miles to work at the grain elevators. Unaware that he was slowly dying of alcohol-induced liver disease. Too poor to be able to repair his television set. Too poor to go to the doctor, although whenever she asked if she could help him out, he always said he was doing okay. And all the time he was sending money to some . . . some leech named Joshua Delaney! Money that could have made a difference in the quality of his own life those last few years!

Her eyes flashing, she grabbed one of the envelopes bearing Joshua Delaney's address and scrambled to her feet. "I'm going to get to the bottom of this. If this man bled Pop dry, I promise you he's about to regret it!"

"Now, kid, maybe you ought to just let things be—"

But Lily Ann was already out the door, her exhaustion overcome by indignant energy.

Three hours later she reached the western city limits of Bartlesville, Oklahoma, and pulled her thirsty, tired Volkswagen in to a service station. All she wanted to do at the moment was sit there and never move again.

She'd noticed while driving that Joshua Delaney's address was on a rural mail route. Finding it could prove tricky, especially since it was almost dark. On top of that, Lily Ann had been at the wheel nearly all day. She'd started out early from Springfield, with only a brief stop at Homer's place, and the miles were catching up to her.

Just then her stomach rumbled a reminder that she hadn't eaten since noon. She was going to indulge in a steak and then get a motel room, she told herself as the station attendant approached. Tomorrow would be soon enough to confront her father's blackmailer.

While the young man filled up her gas tank, she asked him how to find Route Three.

"Piece o' cake!" He gave her a friendly smile, his admiring gaze lingering on her silky blond hair as he related a set of simple directions.

Evidently she was close. Too close to wait till morning, she decided as she paid the attendant.

It wasn't until she followed the highway two miles out of town and located the mailbox, with the address and the name J. Delaney stenciled on its side—it wasn't until she sat staring at the large, attractively rustic, stone-and-timber farmhouse set amid tall pine, elm and native oak trees that Lily Ann stopped to wonder if she might be putting herself in danger.

Hovering there on the side of the road, her engine idling in the late April dusk, it occurred to her that Joshua Delaney could turn out to be one tough character. If he *had* been blackmailing her father, he might be willing to commit violence in order to cover up his crime. He must've had some kind of power to make Ned send him money every month.

Spurred on by that thought, Lily Ann swung her car into the driveway and parked at the front of the house. As she walked up the paved path to the big porch she noticed that it was dark enough by now that the lights should have been on. Was Joshua Delaney away from home, or was he just trying to fool her into thinking he wasn't there?

Good grief, she must be punch-drunk from driving too long! Delaney didn't even know she existed. Why should he pretend not to be at home?

She had just lifted her hand to ring the bell when the house came alive with lights and the door abruptly opened. The sheer unexpectedness of it took Lily Ann's breath away, causing her to gasp even before she saw the man towering in the doorway. And then she swallowed audibly.

Although certainly not a giant, he was tall, perhaps six-two. Lily Ann was five feet seven herself, so she didn't feel small and fragile when facing most men. But *this* man . . . despite his faded jeans and sneakers and the disreputable paint-smeared sweatshirt he wore, there was something about him that made her spring to full attention. It wasn't just his good looks, although heaven knew she'd never before laid eyes on a man so out-and-out gorgeous. It was more that every nerve in her body had begun humming, instantly alert to the disturbing signals radiating out from him. Her senses homed in on overwhelming tension . . . physical strength under rigid control . . . heated undercurrents of anger . . . and most baffling of all, a distinct trace of relief.

Lily Ann took a hurried step backward and acknowledged that she should never have come here alone. What had made her think she could make a blackmailer pay for what he'd done? Joshua Delaney was an unknown force. This place was utterly isolated. Anything might happen here.

She stepped back farther.

"Hey, lady, you can't leave!"

Freezing at the urgent words, she gaped at the man. She was somewhat reassured to see that he hadn't moved an inch, and that he didn't appear on the verge of grabbing her and dragging her inside. But that wasn't what kept her from beating a hasty retreat. No, it was his compelling voice that held her there. Low and resonant, it slid down her spine like a warm, satisfying caress.

Half mesmerized, she had an urge to just keep on staring. There was no denying it: he was truly the handsomest devil she'd ever encountered, his black hair thick and tousled, his face so beautifully sculpted that Kathleen and Dina would have rated him at the top of their hunk scale.

Even in the dim porch light, Lily Ann could see that his nose was prominent, his cheeks lean, his jaw square and determined. Only his mouth hinted at vulnerability with its full, soft lower lip and the tiny indentations at both corners.

His mouth and his eyes, she amended, staring at his half-closed lids and long black lashes. They made him look sleepy. Or maybe he was looking at parts of her that he had no business thinking about.

"Who says I can't leave?" she muttered, crossing her arms to block his view yet still not quite ready to go.

"You're the one who called this morning about the ad, aren't you? You sounded older on the phone. I had just about decided you weren't going to come out today after all." He shifted his stance, keeping one hand on the doorknob. "Don't you want to discuss the job?"

While she didn't have the slightest idea what he was talking about, it occurred to her that this might be a way she could get some information on *him*. "Are you Joshua Delaney?" she asked, just to be certain.

"That's right."

"Well, then, tell me about the job."

He opened the door wider. "Come on inside."

"Thanks, but we can talk right here," she said warily.

He tilted his head as if he were listening for something in the distance. His eyes had inched over to study the lawn, a slight frown tugging his eyebrows together.

Wondering what he found so fascinating, Lily Ann threw a glance over her shoulder but could see nothing remarkable.

"Look," he was saying, his voice taut, "I don't like to leave the children alone. If you'll come on in, I'll check on them. It won't take long."

"The children?" Lily Ann blurted.

His gaze snapped back to her, the lines in his forehead deepening. "The children," he repeated emphatically. "Sarah and Samuel. The reason I have a job for you."

"You want me to baby-sit?" The notion confused her. What kind of blackmailer needed to hire a baby-sitter?

"I want you to watch the children, among other things." He was starting to sound impatient. "Weren't you paying attention when you called? I told you what the job entailed. For that matter, I thought the newspaper ad spelled it out pretty clearly."

Lily Ann didn't plan to go to work for Joshua Delaney in any capacity, so she really shouldn't bother making up believable excuses. But for some peculiar reason, she heard herself stammering, "Well, uh, you see . . . I didn't actually talk to you earlier. That was a . . . a woman I overheard talking in a store. She's the one who saw the ad. She was saying that after she talked to you, she decided she wasn't really interested. And since I . . . I need a job, well, I asked her to give me your address."

For someone who always stuck to the truth, she had come up with a pretty convincing lie, she thought. But before she could figure out whether she felt good or bad about that, she noticed the man's lips compress. "The woman who called . . . she changed her mind about the job because of me, didn't she?" he asked, no longer looking at Lily Ann.

She didn't understand the question or the look on his face. "Because of you?"

"Because I'm blind." He sounded bitter. "She probably assumed it would be a lot more trouble to keep house for me than for someone else."

Wait a minute—because he was *what?*

Something inside Lily Ann rebelled. No way! He couldn't be. He had too much energy. He didn't look blind. He looked . . . intriguing. He looked like a man who knew what he wanted, and who always got it, as well.

"Your stunned silence speaks louder than words. She didn't tell you that part, did she?" His laugh was grim. "So now *you* don't want the job. It looks like you drove out here for nothing. Thanks for your time," he added with thinly veiled sarcasm as he turned away from the front door and started down the hallway.

Still not wanting to believe it, Lily Ann watched him go. Even from her poor vantage point, she could see the golden-haired doll that lay in his path. Some child must have tired of playing and left it lying there amid a heap of doll clothes.

Joshua Delaney stepped on the toy. He probably would have fallen if he hadn't grabbed the corner of an antique desk that sat against the wall and recovered his balance.

There was just enough uncertainty in his movement to convince her. He really *was* blind.

Chapter Two

Lily Ann stood in the open doorway, not knowing what to think. Her illusion that she possessed even a foggy grasp of the situation had just been shattered when Joshua Delaney stumbled.

Could Ned have considered him a threat? He couldn't see! So why had her father been sending him money?

Looking disgusted, the man turned in Lily Ann's direction, then knelt down and swept his hand over the oak floor until he found the doll and its layette. She watched as he silently gathered the mess into his arms and stood back up. When he squared his shoulders and reoriented himself, it appeared that he was about to head on down the hall once more, where only the good Lord knew how many other hazards awaited him.

Lily Ann tried telling herself it wasn't her problem. This man, after all, had somehow intimidated her father. Ned wouldn't have just started paying him off for no reason.

But a nagging doubt chewed away at her indifference, and concern for him prodded her over the threshold. "Somebody needs to teach those kids of yours to pick up their toys, Mr. Delaney. You could have broken your neck."

Despite his unreadable look as he pivoted to face her, she thought he was surprised to discover she was still there. "Sarah doesn't usually leave things lying around," he said. "She understands why she shouldn't."

"Then why did she?" Lily Ann countered softly.

His expression became even more guarded, and his arms tightened around the bundle in a protective gesture. "It's been . . . a little more disorganized than usual around here lately. Both of the children need some time to get over recent changes in our lives."

She wondered how long he'd been blind—if that was one of the changes they were adjusting to—but it wasn't the kind of question she liked to ask.

"Anyway," he went on defensively, "you can't demand perfection from a five-year-old and a child who's not quite four, even under the best circumstances."

Lily Ann wanted to know all about him...not her usual frame of mind when it came to dealing with men, she thought uneasily, but found herself asking anyway, "What about your wife? Can't she keep things picked up for you?"

"If I had a wife, I wouldn't have to hire someone to watch Sarah and Sam," he said and then looked as if he wished that hadn't slipped out. A thundercloud crossed his face, leaving his eyes stormy. They were gray eyes, she could see when he lifted his chin and glared at her with fair aim. Absolutely beautiful gray eyes. "Listen, lady, I don't have time for this, and I sure don't need you to tell me what I'm doing wrong. If you're not interested in the job, then please shut the door on your way out." Taking a step past her, he paused long enough to add, "Just in case you have any bright ideas about making off with the silver, you can forget it. I locked up everything of value when I found out my last housekeeper had sticky fingers."

Lily Ann drew in a stricken breath, not wanting to believe anyone would actually try to steal from a blind man and two small children. Knowledge of some other woman's treachery made it easy to forgive Joshua Delaney's unflattering suspicions about Lily Ann. Instinctive admiration took root within her as she watched him walk on down the hall, his back straight and his head up, until he disappeared through a doorway.

Her expression reflective, Lily Ann went outside and got in her car, then sat there in the dark without starting the engine, her thoughts fixed on the man in the house. She wasn't inclined to leave yet—not while he filled her mind so completely. Part of it was his sheer physical attractiveness; she thought she could have gone on looking at him forever. But it was more than just the outward shell of the man. His pride worried her—his refusal to ask for her help. She found herself wondering what was going to happen next? What if nobody answered the ad? As late as it was getting, it was a safe bet that no one would come out tonight. Had he and the children eaten supper? Could he cook?

Recalling details of his image, it dawned on her that what she had first taken for paint stains on his sweatshirt had in fact been smears of some sort of tomato sauce. SpaghettiOs? Canned ravioli? Was that his idea of good nutrition? How long since he'd done the laundry? No wonder he'd been so uptight when she arrived, and at the same time so relieved. He must have been hoping his search for a housekeeper was about to end.

As if by its own volition her hand reached for the latch and opened the car door. She climbed back out and crossed the yard, then the porch, telling herself that she couldn't very well leave until she got the information she had come all the way from Wichita looking for.

Quietly opening the front door and walking on tiptoes through the hall, she discovered Joshua Delaney in the big, modern kitchen at the back of the house. A kitchen, Lily Ann noted with shock, that looked as if a couple of pre-school-age chefs had been brewing up chaos.

The likely culprits—two small, dark-haired, dirt-smudged kids—sat at the table and listened to the man who stood with his back to them, facing the closet pantry. "I know you'd rather have pizza, Sarah," he was saying, his voice muffled as he fingered the cans lined up on shelves, "but they don't deliver this far out, and I haven't got the hang of the stove yet. Maybe tomorrow."

He was going to master the electric range overnight? Lily Ann wondered skeptically.

"In the meantime," he continued, "we can always heat something in the microwave again."

"Didn't the new lady like it here?" the little girl asked wistfully.

"I don't think so." He stopped exploring the canned goods in order to plow a hand through his hair, his tension obvious in the set of his broad shoulders. "I never should have let her know," he muttered to himself. "It'll only take one slipup when the wrong person's around, and the authorities will be all over us."

At the mention of the authorities, Lily Ann's ears perked up. Was that guilt in his voice? Curiosity got the better of her. "What kind of slipup are you afraid of making?" she blurted.

Joshua stiffened when he heard the young woman's voice and turned toward the doorway, scowling. He hated it when someone sneaked up on him! "You again! I thought you'd be gone by now."

"I started to leave, but then I got to wondering what you planned to fix these kids for supper."

"Nothing that would earn your approval, I'm sure." He stuck his hands into the back pockets of his jeans and thrust out his chin, his mood dark. "Don't you worry about them. They'll get plenty to eat."

"Canned spaghetti again?" she inquired with wry humor.

He didn't see anything funny. "What's wrong with canned spaghetti?"

"Uncle Josh?" a small voice piped up.

Uncle Josh? Lily Ann studied him as he turned in the direction of the little girl. So he wasn't the father of these children? "Yes, Sarah?"

"I'm tired of SpaghettiOs," Sarah was saying.

"Me, too," her younger brother added.

The man tightened his lips and exhaled harshly, flaring his nostrils. "I'm tired of them, too. But you remember what I told you the other day? When I'm fixing supper, we may not always get what we want, but we eat it anyway."

"Yes, sir," the children replied together, sounding so brave and well behaved that Lily Ann wanted to enfold them in a bear hug.

"I wish I could read the labels for you, Uncle Josh," Sarah said. Before Lily Ann could blink away her sudden tears, the child's hopeful gaze slid toward her. "Maybe *she* can read."

"As a matter of fact," Lily Ann admitted, "I can read labels like a pro. But I'd rather not."

"You'd rather not?" Sarah's voice wavered with disappointment.

"Nope! I'd much rather cook something that doesn't come in a can." Lily Ann approached the cluttered table and smiled down at the children. Out of the corner of her eye she could see their uncle, silent and frowning in the background. "And you know what I like to cook best, Miss Sarah?"

Giggling at being addressed that way, the little girl shook her head. "No, what?"

"Pizza."

Sarah's eyes widened. "Really?"

"Really. I promise."

"Pizza! Yea, pizza!" both kids exclaimed, their faces glowing like a couple of thousand-watt bulbs. "Uncle Josh, did you hear—"

"I heard," he cut in dryly, crossing his arms on his chest and leaning back against the pantry door. "Look, Miss—" He broke off. "You never told me your name."

"Lily Ann Jones." She searched his face for a sign that he'd heard it before. Did he know Ned Jones had a daughter? Did he know anything at all about Ned Jones?

"Lily?" He weighed it.

"Lily Ann. I'm named for my mother."

"Mmm. It's nice."

"Thank you kindly, sir. So is Joshua."

"You may as well call me Josh. Everyone else does." Realizing suddenly that her soft voice had distracted him, he gave himself a mental shake. "Listen, Lily Ann, don't let Sarah and Samuel talk you into something if you'd rather not get involved. If there's someplace you have to be tonight—"

"There's not. I'll be glad to check out your pantry and see what I can put together for supper."

"Pizza! Pizza!" Sarah and Samuel chanted until Lily Ann gave a mock groan of surrender.

Reluctant amusement flickered to life in Josh's eyes and curved his mouth. "I believe you did promise."

"So I did. Pizza it will have to be, then. I always keep my promises."

The signs of good humor vanished from his face as suddenly as they had appeared, but he didn't say whatever he was thinking. "Why don't I take the kids and get out of your way?" he offered instead, his tone stiff.

"If it's all the same to you, I could use some help from Miss Sarah and Mr. Samuel," Lily Ann said.

"Please, Uncle Josh!" Samuel begged, jumping down from his chair and running over to tug at the man's hand.

Determined not to let the children be hurt again, Josh knelt down and felt the boy's small warm arms encircle his neck. A second later he felt Sarah embrace him from behind, reaching as far around his shoulders as her arms could go. "Please," she repeated in a whisper that he was afraid Lily Ann could hear. "If we help real good, she might stay."

How in the world could anybody go off and leave these kids? Lily Ann wondered as she watched. The previous housekeeper must have had an ice cube for a heart.

The next instant she felt a surge of foreboding. She had come here to find out what hold Joshua Delaney'd had on her father—not to get involved with him and his family. But she already knew it was going to be hard to walk away. Every time she looked at Josh, her heart felt funny. Maybe she should leave right now, before it got any harder.

As if he could decipher her thoughts, Josh detached himself from the clinging hands and stood up, his mouth as hard as flint. "You can help her make pizza," he told his niece and nephew. "Just don't start believing she'll stay." Turning on his heel, he stalked out of the room.

Lily Ann told herself she would leave as soon as supper was over. It took her a while to locate all the ingredients for a cheese pizza, despite the eager assistance of her two pint-size helpers. While the pie baked and the children stored away every toy that was out of place, she peeled and sliced carrots and cucumbers that she found in the very back of the refrigerator. That done, she mixed up a tasty dip that she hoped would entice everyone to eat the raw vegetables.

She realized very soon that there was no need to entice these kids. In the past few minutes before the oven timer buzzed, Sarah and Sam sat and gazed with longing eyes at the tray of carrot sticks and cucumber slices. Only deeply ingrained good manners kept them from sampling the food before they were given permission.

Lily Ann rushed around the kitchen, loading dirty dishes into the dishwasher and scrubbing every surface in sight as she prayed for the pizza to hurry up and finish cooking. *Poor little moppets*, she thought. They must have been starving!

"When did the housekeeper go away and leave you folks?" she asked as nonchalantly as she could.

"A long time ago," Samuel said.

"It's been days and days," Sarah agreed.

If the cooking utensil she had just washed was any indication, Lily Ann thought it might have been *weeks*. The pot had been sitting on a cold back burner on the stove, with something ugly and congealed in it. Since Josh had said he didn't use the range, the housekeeper must have been responsible for that...that disaster. And to think Lily Ann had first assumed the children had made the mess!

Maybe Josh should just be grateful the wretched woman was gone.

Sarah wrinkled her freckled nose and considered the timing question seriously. "I think it was...maybe...Wednesday. Rena always bought our groceries on Wednesday."

"Did she buy your groceries this Wednesday?" Lily Ann asked, recalling the almost-bare pantry shelves.

"No. She got real mad because Uncle Josh found out she was doing something bad. This time when she went to the store, she never came home."

Samuel looked forlorn as he remembered. "She didn't come to fix our lunch."

"Mildred would never have left us like that," Sarah said matter-of-factly. "Mildred *loved* us."

"Who's Mildred?"

"She was our housekeeper before Rena. Mildred took care of us since Samuel was little. Uncle Josh thought she would stay with us forever and ever. But she died." The child added quickly, "She couldn't help it. She didn't want to die. It was just her time to go." Sarah sounded as philosophical as a grown-up, until she added with a puzzled frown, "That's the same thing that happened to our mommy and daddy."

Lily Ann opened her mouth to say something and found that she couldn't. But Sarah was already moving on to another subject. "Mmm...that pizza smells good! Is it ready yet?"

Switching on the oven light and peering through the glass door, Lily Ann managed hoarsely, "Close enough." She turned off the stove, then slid her hands into padded mitts. "Would one of you please find your uncle and bring him to the supper table?"

"I'm not lost, and I don't have to be brought to the table. I can find it all by myself."

She jumped at the sound of Josh Delaney's low voice behind her as she removed the pizza from the oven. Had he been listening long? Was he angry at the prying questions she had asked Sarah? He might as well get used to it, because she had plenty of other questions that needed answering. The odd thing was, at this point most of her questions had nothing to do with her father.

Hoping to snap Josh out of his touchy mood, she said mildly, "Well, bully for you!"

But when she turned around and saw him, any further quips stuck in her throat. Gone were the grubby sweatshirt and sneakers. He had evidently taken advantage of her time with the children to shower and shave, and he looked so handsome she simply stood and stared.

Josh had donned a pair of crisp, clean blue jeans with a pristine white shirt, gray corduroy sport jacket and polished black boots. His damp, neatly combed hair was starting to curl slightly as it dried, and his dark skin seemed to radiate good health. *Wow*! she thought, dazed all over again by his astonishing good looks.

"Yeah, bully for me." Josh was on edge, resentful of this woman's presence. Annoyed with himself for being so fascinated by her voice. Angry at her assumption that he and the children needed her. A bit depressed because he knew they *did*. "Did you say it's time to eat?"

She cleared her throat, ordering herself to get a grip. "Yes, I did. And not a minute too soon, either. I pity this pizza. Between the four of us, I don't think it stands a chance." She sliced the cheesy concoction into wedges, then put the pan on the table in front of Josh, who had just taken his seat.

After bringing over glasses of water for the kids and iced tea for herself and Josh, Lily Ann pulled out the only empty chair. She winked at Sarah and Samuel and tried to sound relaxed. "Oh, good. I get to sit here by your uncle."

He unfolded his napkin and spread it on his lap, his expression cynical. "Convenient, isn't it? You'll be close in case you have to feed me."

Lily Ann guessed she wasn't the only one who was uncomfortable, which made her feel slightly better. "I hate to tell you this, Mr. Delaney, but you must've got me confused with someone who wants to mother you. Frankly I'm not sure there's enough pizza to go around, and I figured it would be easier to swipe some off *your* plate than off Sarah's or Samuel's."

His eyebrows rose in surprise. Most people had too much respect—or pity—for his blindness to joke about it. Appreciation for Lily Ann's sense of humor drew a short, grudging chuckle from deep inside him. "Don't bet on it, Miss Jones. I'm not as slow as some people think."

If he was talking about Rena, Lily Ann had to agree—his former housekeeper had certainly underestimated Josh. And that wasn't a mistake Lily Ann would make.

Chapter Three

Bong! The grandfather clock struck 1:00 a.m.

Lily Ann lay down on the sofa with a heartfelt sigh and closed her eyes. She had thought she was tired when she first reached Bartlesville—even before that, when she arrived at Homer's place in Wichita. But something had given her the energy to do what needed to be done. Up until now, that is. Now she didn't think she could muster the strength to stir from her comfortable roost.

"I'm just going to lie here a couple of minutes and rest my eyes...." She murmured her apology to the empty living room.

The next thing she knew, she was stretching and yawning, conscious of being pleasantly warm and refreshed. She opened her eyes to find herself snuggled up on a bright floral-print sofa, tucked beneath a down comforter, in a big room awash in sunlight that streamed through a wall of multipane windows. An elegant-looking grand piano sat before the windows in one corner. On another wall, she spotted a TV in one of those big home entertainment centers, but she doubted that it got very much use, since a child's chalkboard stood on an easel right in front of the screen.

To Lily Ann's chagrin, the attractive room seemed only vaguely familiar. The view out the windows showed an expanse of plush green lawn, which she'd never seen before, dotted with giant trees, a picnic table and a swing set, all within the protective boundaries of a chain-link fence. Beyond the fence, rolling green fields stretched for miles.

A small dark-haired girl and boy, both dressed in nice clothes, sat on a bench in the yard and tossed bread crumbs to busy, hopping robins.

The moment she saw the children, Lily Ann's confusion cleared up. This was Joshua Delaney's house! After cleaning this room last night, she had taken a break. She supposed she had dozed off, and while she slept Josh must have covered her up to keep her from getting cold.

"So much for leaving right after supper," she mumbled ironically. Still, she didn't regret having stayed. There was no way she could have gone off and left things the way she'd found them.

Once everyone had eaten all they wanted, she'd restored the kitchen to perfect order, then had gone through the rest of the house like a smoothly efficient cleaning machine, scrubbing, vacuuming and dusting. Most of her effort had been focused on clearing the floor of anything that might cause a blind man to stumble.

Meanwhile, Josh had supervised the kids' baths and put them down for the night on clean bedsheets. Then he'd gathered up the dirty clothes and, with some help sorting things, had started the family's laundry. He'd been working on the last load when Lily Ann fell victim to exhaustion.

Recalling how he had looked carrying Samuel in his arms to bed, she felt a soft smile begin inside her and work its way to her lips. There had been a tautly muscled strength and competence about him, coupled with a gentleness that had touched her very soul. By that time his jacket had been discarded and his white shirt was no longer quite so impeccable. In fact, she had seen a small grubby handprint on his back, where one of the children must have given him a loving pat. They seemed to hug him a lot, but who could blame them? He was clearly the center of their universe.

At one point as she bustled around from chore to chore, she'd been stopped in her tracks in the hallway, captivated by the deep, mellow voice drifting out Sarah's bedroom door. Josh had been sitting beside the bed in the darkened room, telling his niece a story about a little girl who had no friends until she met a donkey. Listening, Lily Ann had felt her heart melt at the familiar portrait of loneliness he was painting with words. She hadn't wanted to budge, at least not until she knew the outcome of the story, but after five hushed minutes of eavesdropping, she'd forced herself back to work.

His voice—or his imagination—had woven a spell around her, she acknowledged the morning after. She didn't begin to understand it, but she guessed it was because Josh was somehow different from anyone else she knew. And she wasn't thinking of his blindness. She wasn't even thinking of his dark, striking good looks or the clean, enticing fragrance she had discovered while sitting next to him at supper.

"Well, okay…maybe I *am* thinking about that, too, just a little," she admitted honestly. But that wasn't surprising, since his delicious scent seemed to emanate from the very comforter that warmed her. He must have brought the cover in here from his own bed when he realized she'd fallen asleep.

"Face it, Lily Ann. You admire him a lot." Her voice sounded deceptively calm, considering that all her instincts were telling her to run just as fast as she could. She didn't *want* to go all weak in the knees over Joshua Delaney, or any other man. Not that Josh didn't deserve her admiration. Anyone with a grain of sense could see how much he adored his niece and nephew, as well as how much patience and fortitude it required for him to care for them by himself. But her respect for his courage didn't account for the warm thrill of pleasure that bubbled through her bloodstream and left her breathless whenever he entered the room. Breathlessness was *not* a good sign, she thought.

To compound the problem, there were still all those unexplained money orders Ned had sent him. She shouldn't get involved until she solved the mystery. Actually she considered herself too smart to risk her heart at all, but her usual trick of turning off her feelings didn't seem to be working this time.

When the chiming doorbell interrupted her brooding, Lily Ann sat up, wondering what was going on. Maybe someone else had called about the job. She probably should have been hoping that was the reason for a visitor, because Josh definitely needed to find a dependable housekeeper. But to her growing dismay, she realized that she was actually unhappy over the possibility of another woman moving in here instead of her.

Instead of her? Wait a second—this must be what it was like to flip out! "How can you even *think* of taking the job?" she asked herself aloud.

She couldn't, of course. She already had a good position in the data processing department of a large insurance company in Springfield. She had worked her way up

in her five years with Nesbitt-Hufnagle, and she wasn't
interested in giving up her job just to become a housekeeper. "Anybody can clean house and watch a couple of
kids..."

Her words trailed off as, through the windows, she saw
Sarah and Samuel jump up from the bench and run toward the kitchen door, where Josh must have called them.
Once they were in the house she could hear them chattering as they went down the hall. Their uncle's distinctive
murmurs accompanied them, evidently encouraging them
to keep the noise down. The sound of his voice made her
pulse quicken.

Oh, no, she thought. This shouldn't be happening! Lily
Ann Jones simply did not make a fool of herself over a
man. She'd better get her rampant hormones under control, and quick!

She heard the opening and closing of the front door,
then the muted sound of a car outside on the driveway.
Deciding to investigate, she threw back the comforter and
slid her legs off the couch. At that point she noticed that
her tennis shoes had been removed and clean, thick socks
put on her feet. Josh's socks, apparently. They were several sizes too big for her, but their woolly softness felt luxurious against her skin.

The idea that Josh had put them on her while she slept
sent a peculiar tremor from her heart right down to her
toes. It felt strangely intimate to be wearing his socks. A
fresh flood of confusion swamped her as she wondered if
he could have used the physical contact to acquaint himself with how she looked. It didn't seem possible for her to
have kept sleeping while he touched her—even if he'd
touched nothing but her feet. Pondering that uneasily, she
wandered into the kitchen.

Josh was listening to the birds rustling and twittering in the eaves, reminded of the last springtime he'd been able to see, the last field of new wheat, the last sunset, when he heard the faint sound of stockinged feet padding along the hall. Shaking off his mood, he turned his face toward the doorway to greet his guest. "Good morning. Did we wake you when the children were leaving?"

Feeling absurdly relieved that Josh hadn't left, too, Lily Ann surveyed him where he lounged casually at the table, a mug of black coffee in front of him. He was wearing a navy blue cable-knit sweater and khaki twill pants that made him look as if he ought to be featured in some stylish magazine ad. She drew a quick mental comparison between his neatness and her own tousled, slept-in state and asked herself what he would think if he could see her.

Nervously she combed a hand through her hair. "I was awake before the doorbell rang. I was just being lazy."

"After the way you worked last night, you deserve to do that." He wore a considering expression. "I've been wondering how I can thank you."

"Forget it." She took a seat across from him. "Believe it or not, I enjoy cleaning house. The bigger the mess, the better I like to get my hands on it. Talk about instant gratification!" Although she spoke lightly, she wasn't kidding. Lily Ann really couldn't stand clutter. As far back as she could remember, messy surroundings had left her with a faint panicky feeling.

When Josh's eyebrows lifted, she forged ahead. "Where did Sarah and Samuel go?"

Whatever he had intended to say, her question made him pause. "A neighbor picked them up for Sunday school and church."

"Ah ha! So you *do* have neighbors, after all."

Although instantly alert, he let her comment pass. "Would you like coffee? Something to eat?"

"I'll have some coffee," she said, starting to push back her chair.

But Josh was already up and heading for the coffeemaker, so she sank back to watch as he took a cup from the cabinet and carefully filled it nearly to the brim. When he returned and set it near her fingertips, she stared at it. "You brewed this yourself? Suddenly I'm not so sure you need a housekeeper."

He sat down again and reached out with both strong-looking hands to find his own mug and wrap his palms around it, his forearms resting on the table. "You put everything back in order for us. I do pretty well when I know where things are." He exhaled, his regret obvious. "Believe me, we still need a housekeeper."

Lily Ann took a sip and found the coffee rich and full of flavor. She savored another taste, then asked, "Exactly how long have you been without help?"

Shifting restlessly, he rubbed one shoulder blade against the back of the chair. "She left on Wednesday."

So little Sarah had been right. "It took just four days for things to fall apart around here?"

Josh hesitated, not wanting to discuss this, then conceded with a grimace that things had been going downhill ever since he hired Rena six weeks ago. "Her housekeeping was pretty erratic, and she wasn't much of a cook. The best thing she did for us was leave."

Lily Ann tried to imagine what it must have been like for Josh to walk through a house where Rena had supposedly cleaned. Anger rose in waves inside her, making her cheeks burn. She didn't like to think about what she would have done had she gotten her hands on the absent Rena.

"Why did you hire her in the first place?" she asked.

Josh smiled a slightly self-mocking smile. "One of these days, Lily Ann, you may find that your options don't always thrill you."

She could guess what he meant. "You hired Rena right after Mildred died?"

His smile grew even more twisted. "So that's what you and my little chatterbox were discussing before supper." He brought his mug to his lips, drank from it and then with measured care set it back down. "Mildred would have been impossible to replace even under normal circumstances. She was like a grandmother to the kids. Within two days of her funeral, I had a social worker breathing down my neck, so I had to hire someone fast—someone who could begin work right away. I couldn't exactly afford to be picky." His shrug conveyed disgust. "When I interviewed Rena, she assured me she could cook a mean pizza."

"In other words, she lied."

When he shrugged again, Lily Ann was possessed of the strongest urge to put her hands up to that lean face and brush back the lock of dark hair that had fallen across his forehead...to tangle her fingers in the silky thickness and learn how it felt...

She stifled the impulse hastily, asking, "What happened to Sarah and Samuel's parents?"

Josh clenched his jaw so hard, a muscle twitched there. Amazing, he thought, that a voice like hers—light, sweet, innocent—could riddle him with pain with just one question. He had to grit out the answer. "When Sam was a year old, they took a second honeymoon, a trip to Hawaii. Their plane went down in the Pacific."

"How awful!" she whispered, watching him lower his unfocused eyes as if he didn't want her to see the grief they contained. Her carefully built-up resistance to him seemed to crumble and fall away as she asked hoarsely, "How long have you had the children?"

It became immediately clear from the way his shoulders stiffened and his eyes snapped open that he had taken the question wrong. "They've been with me from the very start. My brother and his wife named me in their wills to be guardian of their children. I'm their only living kin, but if there had been a dozen relatives to choose from, they would still have wanted me to have the kids."

"Josh, I didn't mean—"

He ignored her protest. "Jeff and I were twins. Our relationship—our ability to communicate—was almost uncanny. After I lost my sight, he and Laura insisted that I come home for a while. This is the house where we grew up, so I never had any trouble finding my own way around. My brother could tell when I was ready to live by myself, to return to my place in Colorado, but I came back here to stay with the kids when Jeff and Laura went on what turned out to be their last trip. They also asked Mildred, who lived up the road, to cook for us and keep things out of my way. After the plane crashed, there was no question of either Mildred or myself leaving." Josh's voice was hard. "Those children are mine now. I'll do anything for them. *Anything*." It was clear that he resented having to justify why he was raising two kids who weren't his own offspring.

Something warm and tender and unfamiliar stirred inside her. "I think you're doing a wonderful job with them, Josh."

"Don't patronize me," he snapped.

"I'm not!"

"Do you mean to tell me you don't have a long list of questions I'll have to answer before you're satisfied that I can be trusted with my own family?"

"Well . . . I wouldn't put it like that. It's not that I don't think you can be trusted, but I have been wondering about a few things—"

"Yeah, I thought so." His mouth tight, he got up and took his cup to the sink where he washed the contents down the drain. "I'd like you out of here before Sarah and Samuel get home."

She gaped at him as he turned back around. "Why? Why can't we talk? I just want to know why your neighbors haven't helped you out until you could hire a suitable housekeeper? If you grew up here, you must know lots of people. I can't believe nobody's been concerned enough to check on you and the kids."

An uneasy look—almost a look of guilt—darted across his features, bringing to mind the words she had overheard him say to himself last night: "All it takes is one slipup when the wrong person's around . . ."

As if a light had flashed on inside her head, Lily Ann suddenly could see: Friends had never helped because Josh had never *let* them help. He'd probably kept people at a safe distance so they wouldn't suspect just what a poor job Rena was doing. But why? Because of his pride? She didn't think so.

Josh leaned one hip against the counter and crossed his arms. "Why should I give you any answers? This is none of your business."

Lily Ann studied him, still working it out in her head. And then it hit her: No matter how invulnerable he appeared, Josh was scared of losing the children.

Oh, dear Lord, of course! It wasn't exactly an unfounded fear, either. Anyone investigating the situation from the outside might just see Josh's blindness and overlook his tremendous strengths. That social worker he mentioned—the one who'd been breathing down his neck—might get so caught up in bureaucratic regulations that the really important issues of love and bonding and family unity would fall by the wayside.

The possibility sickened her. If someone empowered by the state decided he wasn't a suitable guardian, Josh might be forced to give up Sarah and Samuel! She knew beyond a doubt that would be the only blow that could knock him to his knees. And it would just about kill the children to be taken from Josh. At the very least, it would break their hearts.

She couldn't let that happen! But what could she do?

Her thoughts raced in circles, and then a gradual stillness fell over her as the solution crystallized. There was a way she could prevent this family from being torn apart. But the idea left her stunned, afraid.

She held her breath as she wavered, hurriedly weighing the consequences of committing herself so deeply, and the worse consequences if she didn't. After an eternity she swallowed and found her voice. "Don't you think you should be honest with me if I'm going to be working for you?"

The question shook Josh. Had he heard her correctly? Uncrossing his arms, he pushed his hands into his pockets, his posture wary. "What do you mean, if you're going to be working for me? You're not interested in this job."

She swallowed again and managed to speak more firmly this time. "Did I ever say I wasn't interested?"

"You didn't have to say it." He reached up and rubbed his forehead in a gesture of tense preoccupation. "As soon as you found out I'm blind, you couldn't wait to leave."

Stalling, she rose and took her own cup to the sink, then moved to face him. "That's not the way it was at all. I was surprised to discover you're blind, but it didn't scare me off. I didn't leave, did I?"

Josh blinked, and something in his expression made her suspect he'd just become aware of her nearness, her scent. *Let's see how you like it,* she thought with taut amusement. Not just his scent but everything about him disturbed her, which made Lily Ann all the more uncertain that she should be doing this. Josh had the most alarming effect on her!

But she had to put that out of her mind. She had to start thinking of this as just another job. She wasn't going to get hurt—she simply wouldn't let it happen!

He was shaking his head. "I have a feeling you're afraid of my blindness, whether you know it or not."

"I'm not afraid of your blindness," she protested, not pleased that he had picked up on her anxiety. He had it wrong, anyway; it wasn't his *blindness* that bothered her.

"It's nothing to apologize for, if you are. But I can't waste time hiring another housekeeper who won't last—someone who'll run out on us when the going gets rough."

"If I take this job," she assured him grimly, "I won't run out on you. I promise."

"That's just it, Lily Ann. I can't imagine why a beautiful young lady like you would *want* this job."

"What makes you think I'm young and beautiful?" She was gazing down at his socks and wondering again how much he had learned about her when he put them on her feet. At the same time she wondered why in the world she was trying to talk him into hiring her.

His husky laughter relieved a few of the tension lines etching his face, and some of the stiffness drained out of his shoulders. For the first time in weeks, Josh really felt like laughing. "You sound young. And Sarah told me you're beautiful."

Bewitched by his laughter, she drew a shaky breath. "You rely on Sarah for that kind of information, hmm?"

Abruptly he lifted his hands and, without fumbling, placed them on her shoulders. His grip was warm and hard and so pleasant that Lily Ann's heart missed a beat, then began pounding wildly. She stood very still, waiting for him to touch her face.

Josh narrowed his eyes as if that would help him see her, but of course it didn't. It was times like this that he hated his blindness the most. "I take information any way I can get it, Lily Ann." His voice was low. "Look, let's not beat around the bush. Either you want the job or you don't. I need your answer now, and it's important that you're sure of your own mind. I really don't like to play games."

Gazing at his eyes, she felt herself relinquishing all thought of returning to Springfield. In that instant, drowning in a smoky-gray sea, she couldn't remember why she'd ever felt so bound to her job with Nesbitt-Hufnagle. Because it was safe, probably. Safe and controlled and dull. Just like the rest of her life.

It crossed her mind that she had come here to make Joshua Delaney feel sorry for whatever sins he might have committed, not to hire on as his housekeeper, baby-sitter, chief cook and bottle washer. She still didn't know what his relationship had been to her father, and she was going to have to make some effort to find out, because something was fishy. Josh was no innocent. He'd simply gotten under her skin.

And for twenty-four hours a day, every day, she was going to have to be on guard against this man's unconscious charm.

Quite a challenge, she thought. Taking another unsteady breath, she said quietly, "I want the job. I'm sure of it."

Chapter Four

"Did I hear you right?" Homer's voice on the long-distance phone line was so faint, Lily Ann figured she must have thrown him into a state of shock. "You say you're moving down there to work for this Delaney fella? Kid, have you gone off your rocker?"

Lily Ann leaned for support against the brick wall of the convenience store, the pay phone's receiver pressed to her ear. She was still struggling with her own gut reaction to the commitment she'd made that morning. Instinct warned her that emotions she'd always before kept firmly under control had plunged her into a situation she couldn't handle.

Sighing, she suppressed the thought. "It's a long story, Homer. I'll tell you all about it when I make it back to pick up Pop's things. Sorry I forgot the box."

"Aw, you know that's no problem. It can keep on sittin' in the same corner of the closet where it's been since Ned died. What I don't get is what's come over you. When you ran out of here yesterday, I figured you'd have that man behind bars by sundown. Now you're tellin' me you like him so much you want to start cleaning house for him?''

''It's not a matter of liking him.'' *Liking* wasn't exactly the right word. She raked agitated fingers through her silky ponytail, glad her father's keen-eyed pal couldn't see her. He would've known she was hedging. Lately it seemed she couldn't tell the complete truth to anybody. Something kept her from admitting to Joshua Delaney what had brought her to his house in the first place. Nor did she dare let Homer guess just how Josh affected her. The poor old man would worry himself sick about her.

''I sure hope it ain't a matter of you liking him!'' Homer said. ''What do you know about him, anyway?''

''Not a whole lot,'' she admitted. But then, Josh didn't know much about her, either. He was taking a chance, too.

''One thing you do know—he's a blackmailer.''

''I'm not convinced he was blackmailing Pop.'' This much was true. She couldn't be sure until she found some proof.

''Didn't you ask him about it? There was *something* going on. Don't you have some idea what it was?''

''Not yet, but I'll tell you as soon as I know.'' Projecting a self-confidence that was at least half bluff, Lily Ann added, ''Relax, Homer. There's no cause for you to get in a stew just because I've taken this job. I just thought it sounded interesting.''

''But you already have a job.''

''I figured it was time for a change.''

Homer's sniff was dubious. ''You sure you won't think this over before you quit?''

''Too late. I've already called my boss and told him I won't be coming back.'' Ed Carson had offered to hold her position in case she ended up returning to Springfield, but she'd declined. Although his comments about how much he valued Lily Ann as an employee had left her with a warm glow, she doubted if she would miss her computer terminal.

She had called Kathleen next and left a message on the answering machine, requesting that Kath and Dina pack up her clothes and ship them to Bartlesville on the bus when they returned from their camping trip. If they could store the rest of her things so her efficiency apartment could be vacated, Lily Ann would appreciate it. She'd get the stuff out of their way as soon as she could; she promised to write in the meantime and describe this unexpected employment opportunity that had arisen.

She didn't mention Josh, nor did she leave his phone number or address, knowing it wouldn't take much to ignite her friends' curiosity. The last thing she wanted was for those two to show up on the doorstep. Her letter to them would have to be very carefully worded.

After completing that call, Lily Ann had phoned Homer.

"You know, kid, this ain't like you," he said now. "This is more like something Ned would do—up and quit a job for no reason. Go off on a wild-goose chase whenever the notion hit him. Usually ended up sorry, too." He clicked his tongue. "I sure hope you don't get hurt."

When she hung up, Lily Ann stood still as she considered Homer's parting words. She knew she wasn't like Ned. Even as a kid she had fought *not* to be like him—to be reliable and hardworking instead. That was why she had gotten away as quickly as she could. Not that she hadn't loved him. She'd just been determined to escape his influence, and scared to death that if she didn't, she might repeat all of his mistakes.

She could only hope this wasn't a mistake. Josh and the children needed her. If she managed to help them stay together, then she'd be accomplishing what she set out to do. Something told her that was worth any risk.

Temporarily reassured, Lily Ann got back into her car and drove to the grocery store. She consulted her list as she filled a shopping basket, then asked at the front of the store for Bill Akin, as Josh had instructed.

A tall string bean of a man with lank brown hair and eyes that twinkled behind horn-rimmed glasses, Akin turned out to be the store's manager. Upon hearing Josh's name, he took care of everything, ringing up Lily Ann's purchases and putting them on Josh's account, which was evidently settled once a month by a bank officer.

Mr. Akin accompanied her to her car and stashed the groceries in her luggage compartment. "Josh called and told me to be expecting you, Miss Jones. How's he making it? I haven't seen him since Mildred's funeral."

Although the man seemed genuinely concerned, Lily Ann had no idea if he could be trusted. "He's doing fine," she said carefully. "Never better."

"Now that's what I like to hear." Bill grinned, his Adam's apple bobbing and his glasses sliding down his nose. "How're the little tykes?"

"Sarah and Samuel? They're just great."

"I'll bet they are. Those two are about the best-behaved kids around, aren't they?" He opened the driver door for her and then shut it when she had climbed into the VW. Through the open window he added, "Josh is doing a swell job raising them. If other parents gave their kids half the time and attention that he does, we wouldn't have so many problems with young folks today. That's my opinion, anyway." Shaking his head, he chuckled. "I always give Mrs. Ludlow my two cents worth on the subject, but she doesn't seem to listen to anyone who doesn't have a degree in child psychology.''

Lily Ann drove away wondering who Mrs. Ludlow was.

When she reached the farmhouse, she continued on around the side driveway and used the garage-door opener Josh had given her. She parked next to a new-looking, dark red Lincoln in the garage that had been added on to the lovely old house. Unloading the groceries, she noticed how quiet everything seemed.

While she was putting away the milk, she glanced out the kitchen windows into the backyard and saw Sarah and Samuel playing on the swing set. Josh sat on the bench under the trees, his dark head tilted to one side, squinting thoughtfully off into the distance, but whether he was daydreaming or listening to the kids' chatter, it was impossible to tell. He'd changed from the heavier sweater and khakis he'd been wearing that morning into a red polo shirt, white shorts and Reeboks.

Pulled magnetically closer to the window, Lily Ann stared in fascination, thinking how fit he appeared. His sun-bronzed arms and legs contrasted dramatically with the snow-white shorts. She stood watching him until she felt pangs of intense hunger inside her and recognized that it wasn't a hunger for food.

Forcing herself to turn away, she resumed putting up the groceries. By the time she finished, she had persuaded herself that maybe it was an ordinary hunger, after all, since they'd eaten lunch hours ago. Besides, they could all probably stand a cold drink to alleviate the afternoon heat. Quickly she boiled a kettle of water and, while the tea bags steeped, opened a box of snack crackers and spread some with peanut butter. Putting a plate of the small sandwiches on a tray, she added two glasses of milk and two tall iced teas.

Just about ready, Lily Ann thought and dashed into the utility room to glance at her reflection in the mirror over the sink. Her cheeks were flushed, but her ponytail was still smoothly held in place by its clip. If only there had been something more impressive in her weekender case than this simple white blouse and black slacks!

Reality struck with a jolt as she remembered that Josh wouldn't know how she looked. And even if he had known, she should have hoped that he wouldn't be interested. Subdued by the thought, she picked up the tray of refreshments.

Josh started out enjoying the afternoon—relaxed, soaking up the sun's warmth on his bare face and arms and legs while keeping an ear tuned in to Sarah and Sam at play. But after a while the idea that had been haunting him for so long had sneaked back in—the idea he'd tried to exorcise, since he never expected to write another book. By this time he knew the main character well: Baxter Monroe. He could hear his soft New Orleans drawl and picture his rather stooped elegance...could feel his secret rage over the shabby ruins of his life. Baxter was a man of easy external charm who'd been twisted inside by loss and bitterness. A man who craved revenge with every last shred of his sanity.

Strangely fascinating as the topic was, Josh considered it unhealthy to dwell on, even if only for literary purposes. He finally succeeded in blocking out Baxter's obsessive hatred. At the same time he avoided all thought of Rena, as well as of the sozzled bum who had brought about Josh's ultimate undoing at that fateful highway intersection in Kansas. Instead, he propped his back against the trunk of a sturdy elm tree and let his mind drift to a subject he found nearly as troubling in quite a different way.

Lily Ann Jones...a mysterious entity. A lady who'd shown up without fanfare at his door last night, and who in spite of her obvious reluctance had quietly begun taking over the running of his household, smoothing out the wrinkles with admirable proficiency.

What was her problem? Because that special radar of his—his own brand of intuition—told him that she *did* have a problem. The unconscious vibes she sent out were resonant with it: suspicion...guilt...shades of solitary, self-enclosed pain. Beneath all that, he sensed a pull toward him that she was doing her best to resist. Not sympathy, exactly, although he recognized a tender heart when he met one—a soul who meant to help.

No, what she was resisting felt more like the age-old attraction between a woman and a man. If she *was* truly attracted to him, he didn't blame her for fighting it. That was certainly the smart thing to do.

So why had she stayed? And why had he let her stay, considering that he already had all the problems he needed?

From the swing set nearby, Josh heard Sarah issuing bigsisterly orders to Samuel that he should pump his legs harder if he wanted to go higher, and he acknowledged that those two were part of his reason for giving Lily Ann the job. The children had taken to her at once. She could cook—at least, she could make pizza—and the house hadn't felt this clean since Mildred died. Maybe it really would work out, if she stayed long enough. Maybe she'd provide the magic ingredient to convince the woman from social services that the best place for Sarah and Sam was right here with Josh. It was chancy, but it just might work.

As for the rest of his reasons... well, the feelings Lily Ann evoked in Josh had their own undertones of primal, instinctive appeal. He might have lost his vision, but he was still a man, and he hadn't been this achingly conscious of a lady in a long time. It sure stirred him up inside.

He stretched out his long legs and braced himself on both straightened arms, his expression clouding as he tried to imagine what she looked like. The brief times he'd touched her hadn't even begun to satisfy his curiosity. Fitting together the few clues he'd garnered, he deduced that she was tall and slender and fine-boned. Even with no identifiable perfume attached, her scent was essentially feminine, delicate, clean. And her voice was so silky that he didn't care how she looked... he just wanted to listen.

Sarah said she was beautiful. Of course his niece's judgment was questionable, he reminded himself with a grin. Sarah had once suggested that he marry Mildred, who was more than twice his age. But when Kim Newland dropped off the kids this morning, she met Lily Ann and commented, too, on her blond beauty. Kim, a former model, should know what she was talking about.

Beautiful or not, Lily Ann presented an enigma to Josh. It was a little late to be getting cautious, but he knew nothing about her. She didn't strike him as an ordinary housekeeper, and that worried him. If Kael had been in the States, he could have checked her out for Josh. What if she was hiding something? Hiding *from* someone? If she was on the run, the Lord only knew when she might take off again and leave him and the kids in the lurch...

The buzzing whine of the garage door sliding open jerked him to attention. Straightening, he realized with considerable relief that Lily Ann apparently hadn't yet changed her mind about staying. At least he fervently *hoped* that was cause for relief. He half stood as if to go help her carry in the groceries, then grimaced and sat down again. She would have to do it herself; about the best he could do to help was to stay out of her way with the kids.

They also serve who only stand and wait, John Milton had written. Josh frankly doubted if the poet had known what he was talking about, notwithstanding the fact that he'd been blind, too. Endless waiting was just about the most difficult pastime Josh had had to master after the accident, and in his opinion it served no purpose at all.

Nevertheless, he tried to look absorbed in a spring afternoon in the country. The children hadn't noticed Lily Ann's arrival and kept up their chatter, tossing him an occasional question, happy with his preoccupied answers.

The instant he heard the kitchen door open, he gave up acting nonchalant and shot to his feet. "Lily Ann?" He detected a clinking and asked, "What have you got there?"

Josh's perception puzzled and amazed Lily Ann. She was standing on the back step, debating how to shut the door with both hands full. Her hold on the tray was none too secure, which caused the glasses to rattle faintly, and he must have heard the sound.

"I fixed a snack," she said, making a beeline for the picnic table. She plunked down the tray just as Sarah and Samuel shouted a greeting and launched themselves at her.

Samuel threw his arms around her legs in an exuberant hug, while Sarah veered over to grab Josh's hand and yank on it. "See, I was right—she *did* come home! I told you she would!"

Lily Ann lifted a searching look to Josh and saw his embarrassment over Sarah's candid revelation. Evidently it was going to take more than a promise to convince Josh he could count on his newest housekeeper.

"Of course I came home." She tried to sound unruffled. It would never do for him to guess the self-doubts that had plagued her since her decision to stay. He obviously had plenty of doubts of his own. Smoothing Samuel's dark hair, she spoke quietly to the little boy at her knee. "Shut the back door for me, will you please, sweetie?"

As the child raced to obey her, she inquired in a calm voice, "Anyone for refreshments?"

Although her brown eyes lit up at the sight of the food, Sarah kept hold of Josh's hand and guided him to the table before scrambling onto the bench herself. "Sammy's hungry, and so am I. Can we have some, please?"

"You sure can, Miss Sarah." A lump formed in Lily Ann's throat as she realized all over again how much the children and their uncle meant to each other.

A moment later Josh had taken a seat across from his niece and nephew, his fingers laced together loosely on the table in front of him. He listened, his head tilted at an alert angle, as Lily Ann distributed napkins, crackers and milk to the children.

"Here's an iced tea, Josh." She slid the tumbler over until it touched his wrist. "And crackers with peanut butter."

When Josh's hand encountered the cold, moist glass, he curved his fingers around it, out of habit using extra caution not to spill the drink. With his other hand, he found the snack sandwiches and popped one into his mouth. "Mmm . . . Good idea."

As if to underscore his approval, the children dug in with such obvious appreciation that Lily Ann's heart was warmed. She wrapped her arms around her waist and stood watching them eat with more pleasure than she'd felt in ages.

Suddenly she noticed Josh's half-closed gray eyes swing her way. "What's the matter, Lily Ann? Don't *you* like peanut butter and crackers?"

"Oh, sure. Doesn't everybody?"

He inclined his head toward the space next to him on the bench. "Then why don't you sit down and eat?"

It sounded like an order, nicely put. She sat, so nervous at being close to him that she inadvertently poked his broad shoulder with her elbow. *Klutz*! she thought, afraid she would bean him next. Her pulse began to stutter.

Trying to relax, she drew her own glass of tea closer and selected several crackers for herself. But before she could take a bite, Josh shifted his long legs and a warm, powerfully muscled thigh grazed hers, making her stomach contract into a knot of sheer pleasure. Her heart began thudding faster than ever, and her appetite vanished.

All of a sudden electricity seemed to charge the air between them. Lily Ann kept stealing looks at Josh, wondering at his thoughtful silence and the casual way he answered when one of the kids addressed him. She wondered, too, at the stack of crackers that he devoured as he finished off his iced tea. Did he really not notice the electricity, or was his nonchalance a front? She couldn't tell. She was afraid she didn't hide her reaction very well, the sensation of acute physical attraction being so new to her. She had never experienced such exhilaration just from having a man's bare leg brush against hers . . . from inhaling the subtle male scent of him on the soft country air.

One thing she knew for sure—it made her highly uncomfortable. As soon as the children ran to play on the swings again, she inched down the bench and put some breathing space between herself and Josh.

He felt her move away from him, taking her warmth, her delicate essence, her skittishness. She hadn't eaten; she'd just sat there pretending to be comfortable next to him when the truth was, she wasn't comfortable at all. Was her discomfort caused by physical awareness, or something else?

His hands restless, Josh crumpled his paper napkin. "Did everything go okay in town?"

"Yes," she said quickly. "It went fine."

She was studying his profile, admiring it, when she saw a small, vertical frown line form just above the bridge of his bold nose. "Was there a problem with Bill Akin?" he persisted.

"No problem at all. He was very helpful."

Josh looked unconvinced. "You were gone so long, I wondered."

Wanting to reassure him, to erase the worry creases from his forehead, she told him more than she should have. "I wasn't shopping the whole time, Josh. I stopped at a pay phone to make some calls."

He swiveled toward her, still frowning. "You can use the telephone here, Lily Ann. I thought you knew that."

"I...uh, thanks, but they were long-distance calls," she stammered. "I had some, er, business to take care of, and I didn't want the charges to be on your bill." Before he could respond, she stood hastily and gathered up the remains of their food. "I'd better take this inside or we'll start attracting flies."

As she snatched up the tray and left him, Josh clenched one strong hand around his wadded-up napkin, his face tight with speculation. He wondered again what her problem was, and whether she was hiding something that he needed to know. Lord help them, he should have learned his lesson with Rena!

Chapter Five

When Josh followed the children into the kitchen, Lily Ann turned from stirring cinnamon and sugar into the oatmeal, and her eyes widened in silent approval. In his gray dress slacks, white shirt and red-and-gray striped tie, her boss looked like a sleekly handsome businessman getting ready for the office. Had he forgotten to tell her he had a job and needed to be at work today? And why did his niece and nephew look as if they might be going to church again?

"Lily Ann!" Samuel sang out, his grin sunnier than the early-morning sky outside the window. She could tell his dark, baby-fine hair had been combed, despite the unruly tuft sticking up on the crown. Smiling back at him, Lily Ann wondered who had done the combing—the little boy or Josh?

Sarah's curly hair was short enough, with just the proper cut, that she could brush it into perfect order herself. A pink bow that matched her pinafore dress held the bangs back on one side. "You're still here!" she announced with a mixture of relief and satisfaction when she spotted Lily Ann.

"One of these days that will no longer surprise everybody," Lily Ann predicted to the room at large.

Her quip earned a reserved "Good morning" from Josh.

"'Morning, yourself!" she returned, bending to hug Sarah and Samuel before they scrambled onto their chairs. When she stood back up, she found herself within touching distance of Josh, surrounded by his drifting, enticing scent. One deep breath and she felt her knees wobble. A subtle, heart-tugging magic began to envelop her, and a totally uncharacteristic urge came over her to frame his face between her hands and kiss him thoroughly.

Not a smart idea, Lily Ann, she cautioned herself. The thought might be dangerously tempting, but the action was unlikely to be received with any warmth. Josh looked all-business today, and not just because he was dressed like some big-wheel executive. His eyes and mouth showed signs of strain, as if he hadn't gotten much rest last night.

She was pretty sure she knew what had been bothering him; she hadn't slept very well, either. Ever since she cut short their discussion at the picnic table yesterday afternoon, Josh had grown increasingly quiet, an indication that there was something on his mind. Right after supper he'd gone into his study while Lily Ann put the kids to bed and cleaned up the kitchen. Passing by the open door, she had seen him sitting with his elbows propped on the desk, his chin on one hand, eyes fixed blankly on a bookcase full of heavy braille volumes. He didn't seem to have budged from that position when she finally called it a night.

It was clear to her that Josh was having second, and possibly third and fourth, thoughts about their arrangement. They were going to have to talk if there was ever to be any hope that he would trust her.

She watched him touch the table edge with one hand, then use it as a guide to find his chair and sit. Putting a plate of flaky golden-brown biscuits within his reach, she made another stab at humor. "If there's some rule about dressing up for breakfast around here, you forgot to tell me."

The indentations at the corners of his mouth deepened briefly in irritation. "Don't be ridiculous. I have some business to take care of in town." Lifting his head a quarter of an inch, he added, "If you don't mind driving us."

So much for brightening his mood. With a sigh she began spooning the hot creamy oatmeal into bowls. "Maybe I should warn you that all I'm wearing—about the only thing I have to wear—is jeans and a T-shirt...although hopefully a friend of mine will send me the rest of my clothes within a few days."

His thick, dark eyelashes flickered, and his expression underwent an almost imperceptible relaxing. "That's no problem." A gruff quality burred his voice. "I'm sure you look beautiful no matter what you wear."

Such a compliment from a man who'd never seen her had an unsettling effect on Lily Ann, and she stared at Josh as he deliberately dropped the subject. Averting his head, he skimmed his fingertips over his place setting to familiarize himself with the arrangement.

Beautiful? She mulled it over while she put the bowls of hot cereal on the table. The fact was, she used very little makeup, preferring a clean, natural look, and she did nothing to enhance the straight, thick beauty of her long blunt-cut hair except keep it conditioned to a silky shine. Even so, she gave her hair credit for most of the attention that came her way. Blondes just seemed to get noticed more, as Lily Ann had learned in her twenty-four years as one.

But Josh couldn't possibly care whether she was a blonde, brunette or redhead. That realization did something strange to her heart, and she heard an unusual huskiness in her own voice as she said, "If you're sure what I'm wearing is okay, just say the word and I'll drive you clear to Kansas."

His brow furrowed by deep lines, Josh silently reached to find a biscuit. He saw no reason to inform her that hell would freeze over before he ever went back to Kansas.

The moment Sarah and Sam finished eating, Lily Ann sent them to make up their beds and brush their teeth, figuring that would keep them occupied a while. As she cleared the table, she saw that Josh was starting to rise, too.

"Josh, wait!" She deposited the last of the dirty dishes into the sink, then turned toward him. "We need to talk."

A mask of tension clamped down over his handsome features as he settled back in his chair and nodded. They certainly *did* need to talk; he just wasn't sure he was going to like what he heard. "Well? What do you want to tell me?"

"Anything you want to know." She resumed her seat. "I realize you have some questions about my background."

Surprised, he opened his mouth, then shut it again as confusion washed away every other emotion on his face.

"What did you *think* I wanted to talk about?" she asked and then it dawned on her. "Oh, hey, wait! Don't tell me. You expected me to announce that I'm quitting, didn't you?"

But he didn't have to answer; his sheepish look spoke for him.

"I swear, Joshua Delaney! Once you get an idea in your head, you don't give up!" She studied him, half annoyed and half amused. Obviously he didn't know the hold he had over her—that she couldn't bring herself to quit. And maybe it would be just as well if he never knew. "Why would I quit a job I just started?"

In the interval before he answered, she could almost see his uncertainty grow. "Because you've discovered there's too much work to do around here?" he suggested hesitantly.

"I'm not afraid of hard work, Josh."

He couldn't argue with that. He couldn't fault her way with the children or, for that matter, her casual acceptance of his handicap. So far, nothing seemed to throw her, unless perhaps it was when he got too close, either physically or with his questions.

But she had just invited him to ask her anything...

"I am *not* going to quit." Lily Ann's voice was softly insistent.

He rubbed his knuckles along his jaw, considering her reassurance. Instinct told him that she had mixed feelings about working for him, but her promise to stay sounded sincere. "Okay," he conceded, "you're not going to quit."

Blue eyes narrowed, she regarded him carefully but couldn't tell if he really believed the words. "You know, Josh, I understand why you might still have your doubts about my suitability for the position, so let's be frank. What do you want to know about me?"

Josh grunted, thinking that was a tall order. He wasn't quite sure where to begin, but he started with the obvious. "You're not from around here, are you?"

"No. I've been living in Missouri. In Springfield. All my stuff is still there." She gave him a rundown of her employment history, from the salesclerk job she held in high school right down to the name of her supervisor at Nesbitt-Hufnagle.

Josh listened intently, absorbing the details, storing the significant ones in his memory bank while discarding the rest. The fact that Lily Ann had worked in data processing got his immediate attention, and he asked her enough questions about word processing programs to be convinced she knew what she was talking about. He felt a jolt of excitement as an almost undreamed-of possibility struck him.

He rejected the notion at once, refusing to let himself hope. That part of his life was over, and it would do nobody any good to wish otherwise. What he needed to do was concentrate on bringing up Sarah and Samuel in the strongest family unit he could provide, and do his best to repress the creative impulses that had always driven him.

But wasn't it odd that his new housekeeper—the only person even to come about the job—should have all that experience on computers? It seemed as if a divine hand had picked up Lily Ann and set her down right in the middle of his life—a young woman who not only intrigued him with her warm scent and silky voice, but who just happened to possess the skills that could help him resume his writing...

Once more he brushed aside the idea, his face hardening. "How come you aren't working there now?"

"I needed a change...for personal reasons." Seeing Josh's frown she said, "You can call Ed Carson if you like and confirm that he didn't fire me. I didn't pilfer the petty cash or anything. In fact, if I showed up tomorrow wanting my old job back, he'd be thrilled. I was with the company five years, so you can see I don't make a habit of flitting from job to job."

Lacing his fingers together and inclining his head, he appeared to study the lean, taut hands where they rested on the table in front of him. After a minute he lifted his smoky eyes and shifted them in her general direction. "I've known all along you'd never be satisfied working as a housekeeper, Lily Ann. You'll get bored within a week."

She inspected his dark face, acknowledging its profound appeal, then let her eyes drift down his angular, long-limbed frame. Recognizing the courage that had brought him this far, remembering his strength and patience with the children, she felt a tender stirring inside her—a fluttery sensation that seemed to swell and deepen with every beat of her heart.

"I can't imagine getting bored around here," she said a bit hoarsely. "What else would you like to know?"

He thought about pursuing the issue of her being over-qualified for the job, but instead he let it go. If she got bored, he'd find out soon enough.

Okay—what did he want to know? "I've been wondering how old you are," he admitted and when she didn't respond at once, added with a trace of apology, "I wouldn't ask if I could see you. It's just that...you sound so young..."

"What do you mean, young? How young?"

"Twenty-one? Twenty-two?" When she pretended to be insulted, he grinned an engaging grin that crinkled his eyes at the corners and made Lily Ann's heart turn backward flips. "I've been picturing you as fresh out of college, but that can't be true if you've been with Nesbitt-Hufnagle full-time for five years. How far off the mark am I?"

"I'm twenty-four, so you're not too far off, actually." She spoke forgivingly. She would have forgiven him just about anything, as long as he smiled that way. "Except that I never got very far in college."

"Why not?"

"I couldn't afford to stay in school if I wanted to eat and pay the rent. So when I was nineteen, I went to work for Nesbitt-Hufnagle."

Josh absently scratched one eyebrow. "Where does your family live?"

Something inside her tensed. "I never had any brothers or sisters, and my parents are dead." The image of Ned that flashed through her mind left her shaken and with an unaccountable impulse to steer Josh in another direction. "How old are *you*, Josh?"

From the frown that drew his eyebrows together, she could see that he wasn't overjoyed at handling curious inquiries about himself. He probably anticipated being called upon to explain the circumstances of his blindness, or something else that he considered off-limits. After a conspicuous pause he said succinctly, in a tone meant to discourage further probing, "Thirty-four."

She nodded to herself, patient enough to dole out her questions as he would tolerate them. But there was one thing she was dying to know...

"So," she said with assumed nonchalance, "how else have you been picturing me...besides young and well educated, I mean?"

His expression changed, softening as the frown lines smoothed out and a half smile curved his mouth. "I know you're a blonde," he said, to her extreme surprise. "And beautiful. At least that's what everybody tells me."

"Everybody like Sarah, you mean?"

"Mmm. And Kim Newland, the neighbor who brought the kids home from church yesterday." His smile widened. "Samuel mostly just talks about your cooking."

"In complimentary terms, I hope?"

"Oh, yes!" His wry assurance reminded her that after eating SpaghettiOs for several days, all three of the Delaneys must have considered Lily Ann to be a veritable Julia Child.

"That's good. I'm glad he approves. Uh, Josh...I'm not exactly gorgeous, you know. I'm really pretty ordinary."

He tilted his head as if he were looking right at her, raising one eyebrow quizzically. "Is that right?"

"Yes. I...I just thought I should be honest about it."

"I appreciate your honesty," he said with a straight face, in a voice that was as dry as dust.

"Yes, well...was there anything else we needed to discuss?"

"We probably ought to reach some sort of agreement about your salary, don't you think? We'll be seeing my banker in town, and I have to tell him how much to pay you."

Lily Ann wondered what Josh's stuffy banker was going to think when she came in wearing jeans and tennies. Her next thought was amazement that she had never asked what she'd be earning at this new job. The issue of salary hadn't even occurred to her! Not that it mattered. She'd already established in her own mind that she was fully committed to keeping Josh and the children together, and the size of her take-home paycheck wasn't going to change that.

But what if you discover that something awful was going on between Josh and Ned? What if Josh really is a blackmailer? Or...what if Ned owed Josh—owed him big time?

She sucked in her breath and clenched her hands on her lap, trying with only partial success to wipe her mind clean of the questions that had just intruded. "Okay, let's discuss my salary," she said nervously. "How much am I worth?"

Josh's lips formed a slow, thoughtful smile. "I couldn't even begin to calculate what you're worth, Lily Ann. But here's what I can pay you." He named a figure that got her attention in a hurry. It was almost as much as she had made in Springfield . . . and Josh was also providing room and board. "Is that agreeable?"

"Sure!" She'd have to be crazy to argue.

"That's settled, then." He pushed back his chair and stood up. "How soon can you be ready to leave?"

"You're the boss. You say when."

He nodded. "I'll meet you at the car in five minutes. You bring the kids."

She watched him head for his bedroom, all the more pleased to see his long-legged stride because she knew he didn't always walk so confidently. At the same time she felt uneasy in ways she couldn't comprehend.

Chapter Six

Having spent too many years driving a VW bug that had seen better days, Lily Ann felt a little out of her league behind the wheel of Josh's Lincoln. But he'd insisted, and Josh, in business suit and with briefcase in hand, looking heart-stoppingly handsome, was not one to be dissuaded once his mind was made up.

"It would be more economical to take my car," she had pointed out. "I've got a full gas tank—"

"Thanks for offering, but I don't think we'd all fit in your Volkswagen. I know my legs wouldn't." He'd helped Sarah and Samuel fasten their seat belts, then had shut the back door and climbed in front himself after sliding the briefcase to the middle of the broad seat.

She had to admit there was still plenty of room on the soft leather seat for her, as well as space on the plush carpeted floorboard for him to stretch out his long legs. A bit awed by the luxurious comfort, she made no further protest, although as she pulled out onto the highway she said a silent prayer that she wouldn't dent or scratch Josh's car—or Josh and the children, she added fervently when that horrifying possibility dawned on her.

But the Lincoln handled like a dream, and Josh apparently had faith in her driving skills, judging by his relaxed posture. She was glad they'd had that talk after breakfast, because it seemed to have relieved his doubts. He wore a look of thoughtful amusement as he listened to Samuel chattering happily to himself.

By the time they'd reached the Bartlesville city limits, Lily Ann's own confidence in her driving was restored and she had loosened up enough to broach a subject that was bothering her. "Uh, Josh, about my salary..."

He turned his head slightly. "What about your salary?"

"I've been thinking...are you sure you can really afford to pay me that much? I mean..." This was awkward. "Well, you don't have a job, do you?"

"A job? No." One corner of his well-shaped mouth slanted up while the other was being tugged down, making it hard to tell whether he was fighting a smile or a frown. "That's not bad in and of itself, Lily Ann. Some people aren't cut out for a nine-to-five job."

How well she knew that from observing her father! "I realize what you're saying is true, but..."

"But I'm blind, which must mean I'm destitute as well?" His features had just settled into a full-fledged frown.

"That's not what I meant. I just thought...it would be okay if you paid me less. I could get by. Maybe that way your money would stretch farther."

"Don't you worry about stretching my money." His tone conveyed the chilly impression that how he spent his money didn't concern her.

Shifting abruptly on the seat, he opened the briefcase, took out a white stick, not much longer than a ruler, and slapped it down on his lap. If his short movements as he closed the case and faced the front were any indication, Lily Ann thought she must have offended him. Why hadn't she kept her mouth shut and just enjoyed the smooth way things were going? Now she'd spoiled his mood.

Her heart sank, then sank a little lower when Sarah inquired, "What's a desitoot, Uncle Josh?"

"Destitute?" His long fingers curled around the stick until the knuckles turned pale. "It's not a thing, Sarah—it's a condition. It means broke. In need of charity."

"Broke like your eyes?"

At the little boy's innocent question, Lily Ann clutched the steering wheel, feeling a stab of anguish.

"No, Samuel." Josh's response was level. "Broke can also mean poor, not having any money."

"Like the starving little babies in Africa," Sarah explained to her brother. "Remember how they take up a collection at church to send food?"

"Oh, yeah! I gave all my 'llowance," Samuel said.

"Uncle Josh? Are we poor?" Sarah sounded more curious than anxious, but Lily Ann groaned silently. How could she have started such a loaded conversation? She was supposed to make the children feel *more* secure, not less!

"We aren't poor in any way that matters," Josh said firmly, "and don't believe anybody who tries to tell you otherwise."

His niece seemed glad to leave it at that, and so, for that matter, was Lily Ann. Still, she decided gloomily, she *had* offended him. From now on she'd be careful to treat him the same as she would treat a man with perfect vision.

But could she do that? she wondered when she had located the bank and parked the car. The fact was, people who couldn't see were bound to need help from time to time.

Jumping out, she opened the rear door and leaned in to unbuckle the children's seat belts, then assisted them from the car. She stood with an arm around the shoulder of each child, watching Josh pull out the briefcase and straighten to shut his own door. Should she take his hand, or take Sarah's and Samuel's?

Before she could do either, Josh gave his wrist a snap, and the white stick he was holding unfolded with a couple of clicks into a thin cane three times its original length. The next thing she knew, he was making his way to where she waited with the kids.

"You lead," he said in that same even tone that told her absolutely nothing of what he was feeling. At least he didn't really sound mad. "It helps if I can hear you, so I know I'm headed in the right direction."

"Okay." She reached down and clasped Sarah's and Samuel's hands, but even as they crossed the parking lot and approached the main bank entry, she watched Josh like a hawk, worried he would get separated from them.

But Josh clearly knew the route well. He steered a straight course down the sidewalk, detecting and avoiding the flower bed that edged the walkway, despite Lily Ann's fear that he would catch his foot on the raised brick border and tumble headlong into the rosebushes. Opening the heavy glass door for the others, he informed her that their destination was an office at the left front of the lobby.

It was Josh who greeted the secretary, and Josh who instructed the children to sit down and mind the motherly Mrs. Zimmerman. And when the vice president escorted them into his office, it was Josh who introduced Lily Ann to Grover Thomason.

The banker was around Josh's age, half a foot shorter and twenty pounds heavier. From the sound of their banter as he settled Josh and Lily Ann into comfortable chairs, she thought the men's friendship must have gone way back.

Mr. Thomason was hardly the stuffy bank executive Lily Ann had anticipated. Paying no heed to her casual attire, he urged her to call him Grover and remarked that she was by far the prettiest nanny he'd ever met. After offering his guests coffee, which they declined, he put Josh's briefcase on the desk. "Let me take a look at your mail."

Five minutes later he had separated the week's correspondence into several stacks and was looking somber. He exhaled deeply, then asked Josh if he preferred to discuss his business in private.

Despite Grover's affability, Josh had sensed his tension ever since entering the office, and the vibrations intensified now. "Why? What's wrong?"

"Nothing you didn't warn me to be expecting." Grover smoothed his thinning hair.

"My former employee ran up some unauthorized bills?"

"Unless you've taken to wearing gold chains and silk stockings."

Fidgeting, Josh leaned back in his chair. "Can you make sure it doesn't happen again?"

"As of today nobody charges anything to you without either your approval or mine. Also, I've advised every business where you have an account that they'll need to get clearance on the amount and nature of each purchase."

Josh was less than thrilled. "I guess that'll work."

"Blast it all, Josh!" Grover exploded suddenly, his manner agitated. "This shouldn't have happened. If I had—"

"Hold on." Josh extended one hand. "It wasn't your fault. Don't take it so hard, Grover. She didn't do any permanent damage. Anyway, it could have been a lot worse."

"Yeah," the other man muttered, "she could have been an ax murderer."

Josh heard Lily Ann's soft gasp nearby and, even though he knew Grover meant well, wished he could muzzle his old friend. He'd already spent sleepless nights agonizing over what Rena *might* have done; now he just wanted to put the entire episode to rest before Mrs. Ludlow came snooping around again. Forcing a note of humor he said, "Your imagination's running wild, Grove. You haven't been watching scary movies on television again, have you?"

Grover started to say something, then stopped and grinned reluctantly. "I've been reading scary books. *You* know the kind."

Lily Ann wondered at Josh's wry nod and concluded that this must be a private joke between the men.

"Okay, then." The banker had calmed down. "I'll see that these bills are paid, as usual. There's some personal mail that you'll want to hear and answer. Would you like me to read it to you?"

"No, thanks. Lily Ann can do that at home."

"Okay." Grover flipped through a stack of papers, appearing to search for something, then put them aside and shook his head. "Once again, there's no money order. You sure you didn't have it out with the old coot?"

Talk of money orders snapped Lily Ann back to full attention just as Josh said curtly, "I'm positive."

She wanted to know *what* money orders—and what old coot—Grover was referring to? What had Ned been up to?

"Hmm. Well, I can look into it if you like—find out what the problem is."

Josh managed to glare quite effectively, despite the fact that he was somewhat off in his aim. "What I'd like is for you to forget the whole thing. Permanently. I never wanted the money in the first place."

"Yes, you made that clear! I never understood why you wouldn't keep it. You deserved a lot more, after what..." He stopped with a glance at Lily Ann's wide-eyed face, then shrugged. "Anyway, the church put it to use stocking the soup kitchen, so at least some good came of it."

When Josh made no response, Grover rubbed his hands together and picked up the last pile of mail. "Now we're down to the juicy stuff. There are some hefty checks here from your publisher. The royalty statements indicate continued strong foreign sales for your last four books, particularly in Japan and Spain. Phillip McKay stuck in a note for you, sending his regards. He thought you should be aware that thanks to the opening up of eastern Europe, they're translating all your work—including your earlier books—and planning a big promotional campaign in the new markets. He thinks Cole Delaney will be an instant hit over there..."

The moment Grover mentioned royalties, he lost Lily Ann completely. He seemed to be implying that Josh was a published author, and a successful one at that—a concept that momentarily made her forget money orders and Ned. She hadn't had a clue that Josh's past had included anything other than some perfectly ordinary occupation.

And then Grover spoke of Cole Delaney, and her confusion grew. This was an author she knew! He wrote books that made the bestseller lists. Books with exciting, intricate plots and unforgettable characters. Novels that delved into the quirks of the human psyche and played on the reader's own fears and fancies to create often humorous, sometimes terrifying, but always fascinating adventure yarns with a moral. She'd read several of his books herself, although she didn't think he'd written anything in years.

Was she crazy to imagine it, or could Cole Delaney and Joshua Delaney really be one and the same?

"...just got back from his vacation in Great Britain, so you can expect Phillip to call you any day now," Grover was saying when Lily Ann struggled out of her daze. "He has some ideas he wants to run by you."

"He always does," Josh said with a grimace. Phil called him periodically, partly to keep in touch as the caring friend that he was; however, as an editor, he was always prodding Josh to come up with a book proposal. Phil simply wouldn't take Josh's word for it that his writing career was finished. At least, he hadn't taken his word for it yet, although at some point even the invincible Phillip McKay would have to give up.

Sensing Lily Ann's dumbfounded interest, Josh clenched his jaw. "Is there anything else in the mail?"

"A check from your stockbroker and also one from the petroleum company. I can see these are prosperous days for you oil barons."

Oil barons? Josh's income included money from stocks and oil? It certainly appeared so—a *lot* of money, from the looks of the vouchers. And she had thought he might have trouble paying her!

"Why don't you take these to Mrs. Z and have her deposit them?" Grover put them in Josh's hand. "Meanwhile, I can work out arrangements with Lily Ann concerning her salary."

Josh looked reluctant to leave, but he stood, picked up his cane and went, while Lily Ann stared after him, numb with shock.

Once the door closed, Grover's smile faded and he turned bluntly to her. "I'd like to see your driver's license for identification. Then I'm going to call your last employer for a reference." He gave her a challenging look, which she ignored. She wouldn't have protested even if she'd had the energy.

Thomason seated himself behind the desk and, with grim concentration, copied the information from her Missouri license, all but studying the photo with a magnifying glass. Then he dialed Nesbitt-Hufnagle in Springfield and spoke to Ed Carson, asking probing questions of her former employer.

Finally satisfied, Grover hung up and did all the paperwork to open a bank account for her, obtaining her signature on numerous forms. Her salary would be deposited directly from Josh's account into hers, Grover advised her, according to whatever schedule she preferred—weekly, biweekly or at the end of each month of employment. She chose to have it done monthly.

To cover any expenses before her first paycheck, Lily Ann wrote a check on her Springfield bank to be deposited in Bartlesville. When Grover asked her to name an account beneficiary, she didn't have to deliberate very long. "You might as well put Josh down. I don't have any family." Reminded of Homer, she added him as cobeneficiary.

As he finished up, the banker's expression softened. "You do understand that I had to check on you? Josh is a good friend—a terrific guy—and he's been through hell."

She met his gaze with a direct stare of her own. "If you hadn't cared enough about Josh and the children to do this much checking, I don't think I could ever trust you," she said.

Looking relieved, Grover excused himself to have a staff member finish opening the account and a few minutes later returned with a packet of temporary checks for Lily Ann. "All set," he said, handing her his business card. "Keep this and call me if any problem ever comes up, day or night. My home phone number's on the back." He added gravely, "I'm afraid Josh is reluctant to bother people. He's got too much pride. But don't you be afraid to call if he needs something... or if you or the kids need anything. That's what friends are for."

Josh didn't say much during the drive home, but then the rest of them were quiet, too. The children had lollipops, courtesy of Mrs. Z, to keep them occupied, and Lily Ann was busy trying to sort out everything she had discovered. She'd learned things about Josh that boggled her mind, and she suspected there was much more still to know.

"Can we go swing?" Sarah asked as they were getting out of the car.

"Change your clothes first," Lily Ann answered automatically. "Put on play clothes, and hang up what you have on now. I'm proud of you both for not getting dirty." As they skipped on ahead of the adults into the house, she called after them, "And stay inside the fence!"

Josh wore an abstracted look when he followed Lily Ann into the kitchen. He had already taken off his suit coat, and now he set his briefcase on a chair and laid the jacket across it, then reached up with his free hand to loosen his tie. The other hand still held the cane, which he had folded.

Watching him, she blurted, "I'm sorry, Josh."

He didn't move for a moment, then placed the cane on the edge of the table, his profile turned to Lily Ann. "Why should you be sorry?"

"Because I bungled things all the way around. I...I guess it wasn't very diplomatic to suggest that you couldn't afford to pay me. The last thing I meant to do was offend you, but I just..." She stopped, unable to tell him how she had felt thinking it might pose a hardship on him.

A slight smile curved his lips at her apology. He hadn't remained offended very long. Stung pride had given way to amazement that she was volunteering to take a pay cut. Rather than being greedy for more of his wealth, she was willing to take less! Unlike Rena, Lily Ann hadn't had any idea that she could profit from working for Josh; she had simply been there to help him, even if she wasn't exactly sure how to do that.

"You were concerned about us—Sarah and Sam and me. That's no reason to apologize, Lily Ann."

"There I was, talking about your not having a job, when in reality I guess you're rich, or almost. Rich and famous." She paused a moment. "You *are* Cole Delaney, aren't you? I mean, you write under that name?"

"I used to." He moved to face her more fully. "Cole's my middle name...my mother's maiden name. She died when I was eight, but she'd already taught me to love books."

"So you took that as your pen name to thank her?"

"That and to avoid any possible complications on my job," he agreed, nodding. "When I first started writing, I was working in the field of psychology." The grin he flashed held a bit of sheepish devilry. "I didn't think the mental health agency would be pleased to have one of its therapists make a name for himself writing psychological thrillers."

She could see his point. "Well, you made a name for yourself, all right! I just didn't know who you were."

"There was no reason you should have known, was there?"

"Maybe not, but I must have looked like an idiot this morning. I felt like one, anyway."

"Trust me, you don't look even remotely like an idiot." He spoke dryly. "You look like a golden-haired angel with eyes the color of a summer sky."

"Sarah again?" she demanded, feeling out of breath. Josh seemed to be coming closer all the time, although she wasn't sure which one of them had moved.

Still smiling, he shook his head and extended both hands in a cautious searching manner to touch, then span, her waist. She was slim and just the right height, as far as he was concerned. He felt an ache inside him, a yearning to see her. "Not Sarah this time. Grover." His smile faded. "Grover was worried when he first met you—worried that you weren't what you appear to be. I didn't know if he would call the police on you while I was out of his office."

A pleasant tingling sensation spread from where his lean hands rested on her. "It would have been okay, Josh," she said shakily. "I'm not hiding a criminal past."

He tightened his hold and pulled her closer to his tautly muscled length. "I know that. But Grover's been giving me a hard time about not reporting Rena." Bitterness laced his voice. "He doesn't understand the ramifications if child welfare hears about it and gets to thinking I couldn't protect the kids from my own housekeeper."

"Nobody's going to take Sarah and Sam away from you. I promise you that."

He heaved a quiet sigh. "I wish I could believe your promises."

She slid her arms around him. "You can trust me."

"That's what Grover said, after he talked to you alone for a while. He also said you're beautiful." Josh hesitated, his lashes dipping down to obscure the mystery in his eyes. Even so, gazing up at him, she saw frustration glittering there, and a silvery spark of defiance. His voice dropped. "I'm tired of hearing about your beauty. I want to discover it myself."

Deliberately, carefully, he lowered his head until his mouth touched her forehead. A second later he buried his face in her hair, nosing into the silky fullness. Over the pounding of her heart, she could hear him draw in long, hushed breaths. "You smell wonderful, Lily Ann—like roses and sunshine after a rain."

Something dragged the truth from her. "Oh, Josh—you smell so good it frightens me!"

Feeling a powerful release, he took his right hand from her waist and slid it upward, his palm grazing her arm and shoulder. When he reached her throat, his long fingers curved against her warm skin and rested there briefly, his thumb pressed to her throbbing pulse point as if measuring her reaction before moving up to her face.

Once there, deft fingertips glided over each feature, his touch feather-light yet gently provocative...more provocative than she could have believed before he set his hand loose on her. By the time he had finished exploring her loveliness, she was lost in a haze of indescribable joy.

When he rubbed the pad of his thumb across her parted lips, she gasped, swallowed and kissed his thumb. Josh shivered at the kiss, then wrapped her in both arms, bending his head and following the curve of her cheek to her mouth. His lips brushed back and forth like velvet sandpaper and then clung to hers while she melted inside.

He released her much too soon, and yet not soon enough, because when he lifted his head, she knew with a terrifying certainty that she would never be the same. He had changed her irrevocably—given her a hunger for something that could never be hers.

"They were right," he murmured rather thickly.

"Who?" she managed.

"Sarah. Grover. Kim Newland."

He didn't say anything more, but he didn't have to. Lily Ann knew what he meant: he found her beautiful, too. And he didn't sound any happier about his discovery than she felt about hers.

Chapter Seven

Lily Ann ran her cleaning rag over the dark oak desk in the study, gazing around with pleasure as she worked. She associated the comfortable room with Josh, because he spent so much time in here when he wasn't with the children. The thick gray carpeting and book-lined walls seemed to insulate it, making it quieter than anywhere else in the house, and the plump-cushioned sofa invited a person to let the world pass by while they curled up with something to read. Something like one of Cole Delaney's novels. She'd just finished rereading the first in her spare time and could hardly wait to take down the next from the bookshelf and get started on it.

Of course, many of these shelves held material that she couldn't decipher at all. She stopped dusting the computer monitor long enough to thumb through the big braille volume that lay open on the desktop. It was a thesaurus, according to the printed cover, and for all she could make of the pages, it might as well have been Greek.

No doubt Josh had been looking up some word in it...but why? Was he mentally composing something? A letter, perhaps? He'd gone over his mail with Lily Ann when they returned from the bank on Monday and she thought he'd dictated all the responses he intended to send.

A day or two later his editor had called and talked to Josh about starting a new project. Lily Ann knew that because she'd inadvertently overheard Josh tell the man not to be ridiculous—how on earth was he supposed to think about writing a book when he had a list as long as his arm of things that needed his attention around here? He'd sounded good-humored if somewhat tongue-in-cheek when he said that, but later she had seen him sitting at the computer, with the power turned off as it always was. He'd been fingering the keyboard, his expression brooding and restless. It was pretty clear that, unlike Lily Ann, Josh dearly missed his computer terminal. And unless his PC was the kind that could speak, she didn't see any way he could operate one.

But at least he could use the stove now, if the need arose. Tormented by even the remote possibility that Ned had had a hand in ruining Josh's life, Lily Ann had racked her brain to come up with ways to open doors that had been closed to him. Not knowing what reaction to expect, she'd offered to explain the controls on the electric range to him. Evidently he never wanted to find himself dependent again, because he accepted her offer.

"I used to cook occasionally before I moved back here from Colorado," he said as his hands examined the knobs and their corresponding burners. "I always meant to ask Mildred how this one works." A moment later he muttered with irony, "Have I told you she wasn't supposed to die?"

With every shred of her strength Lily Ann fought the tender emotions she was feeling and came up with the practical suggestion of labeling the items in the pantry with plastic tape. An alphabet punch marked the tape with raised letters, which Josh could read with his fingertips. Just to show that he could, he made macaroni and cheese for dinner one evening—a simple meal that proved enormously popular with the kids.

"I like Lily Ann's cooking," Sam confided to his uncle as Josh tucked him into bed that night, not aware that she was listening at the door, "but you don't make vegetables. Could you cook again tomorrow?"

When the children were asleep, Josh and Lily Ann laughed together over that, and her breath caught in her throat at the sight of his free and easy amusement. His dark head was tilted back, his cheeks creased, white teeth gleaming in a wide grin, eyes crinkled up at the corners— the whole works. It was enough to melt her on the spot. Josh in any kind of mood at all could make heads turn, but Josh laughing could stop hearts. And Josh's kiss . . .

Resolutely she banished the thought of the kiss they'd shared. She had made up her mind to forget it had happened—just as she wanted to erase Grover's enigmatic comments about the money orders—but forgetting something as impressive as that kiss was turning out to be easier said than done. Half of her time seemed to be spent in trying to ignore the evocative memory, the other half in wondering if there would ever be an encore performance.

She finished dusting the furniture, then checked her watch and realized the pot roast would be done in ten minutes. She'd better set the table and get ready.

Get ready to sit next to Josh, an inner voice warned her with a shade too much buoyant anticipation for her peace of mind.

"Get ready to have your willpower tested," she mumbled aloud, thinking that her willpower hadn't always been so wimpy.

"Let's not tear down our sand castle," Sam said when Josh suggested they'd better go inside and clean up for supper. "Let's leave it for Lily Ann to see."

"She'll be totally amazed, Uncle Josh!" Sarah assured him.

Barefoot and on his knees in the sandbox, where he'd spent half the afternoon, Josh patted the lopsided structure, feeling the toothpick-flagpoles on its towers and the crayon-cannons the children had positioned around the top to protect the fortress. He disciplined his grin and inched backward until he figured he could safely get to his feet without tripping over one of the architectural wonders of the world.

"I'm sure she will be," he agreed, dusting his palms together. "Okay, the castle can stay." He held out one hand. "Where'd you put my cane?"

"Here." Samuel handed him the stick, and the three of them started across the yard to the house.

"Did you guys brush off the sand?" he thought to ask as they stepped inside the kitchen door. The mouthwatering aroma of old-fashioned pot roast assailed him so he almost missed the answer—or rather, answers—to his question.

"Yes, sir," Sarah and Samuel said in chorus at the same time that Lily Ann gasped and blurted, "No!"

Josh froze at the urgency in her voice. Painful experience had conditioned him not to move when someone spoke to him in that tone.

"Good grief, what have you been doing—burying each other in the sandbox?" Lily Ann saw Josh's features relax as it dawned on him what she'd yelled about. With mock severity she added, "Never mind, don't tell me. And don't any of you take another step, or I'll have to clean the house again. Wouldn't you like us to get around to eating sometime tonight?"

The children looked alarmed at the possibility of not eating. Josh merely looked sheepish.

"Come on, let's go back outside and empty your pockets and cuffs. I swear, we could probably create our own beach in the middle of the kitchen floor if you three gave yourselves a good shake."

After duly admiring the sand castle that had caused all the trouble, Lily Ann ended up stripping the shorts and T-shirts off of Sarah and Samuel and sending them in to rinse off in the shower. Then she turned to survey Josh and her pulse automatically shifted into high gear.

"Am I next?" he asked innocently, one eyebrow lifted.

"Mmm . . ." Flushed and breathless, she was almost excruciatingly conscious of his brown, well-muscled body in the black-and-tan striped knit shirt and khaki shorts he was wearing. Even his sun-bronzed, sinewy feet appealed to her. "You must be. I don't see any other customers."

She began gingerly brushing off the grains of sand that clung to his clothes and warm skin, chewing her bottom lip as she worked. It was difficult to be matter-of-fact about touching him when she had made a point of coming into actual physical contact with him as little as possible for five whole days. But she tried.

Meanwhile, he stood patiently, his mouth quirked in a half smile that could have meant just about anything.

"Almost through," she said. "How about bending over?"

Obediently he leaned forward from the waist and braced his hands on his knees. Lily Ann threaded her fingers into his hair and ruffled it, combing through the jet-black thickness several times to be sure she got rid of the gritty sand.

In truth, there wasn't all that much sand in his hair, but she didn't want to stop. His hair felt like satin and curled around her fingers with a delicious intimacy that made her shut her eyes briefly in undeniable longing.

"You need a trim," she murmured without thinking when she had finished.

He straightened up and ran his own fingers through his hair, taking measure of the shaggy neckline. "Yeah, I guess I do." He looked thoughtful. "It's been a while since haircuts were very high on my list of priorities." His right hand, flattened, swept down the front of his clothes in a perfunctory, searching gesture. "Is it safe to let me in the house now?"

Detecting a wry note in his voice, Lily Ann tore her attention from the width of his shoulders and glanced up at his eyes. It jolted her a bit to find them half-closed and unfocused rather than meeting hers with a glimmer of sardonic humor. Her stomach clenched at the reminder that he was blind.

"I think it's safe," she said huskily and watched him reach for his cane where he'd propped it against the side of the house. "Josh?" He stopped and waited. "If you like, I could give you a haircut after supper."

Whatever had made her suggest a thing like that? she wondered the moment she'd uttered the words. Just how far did she want to push her willpower?

Bending his head, he considered her offer. "You do haircuts, too, hmm?"

"Well…I'm not a professional. I've never been trained or anything."

His lips twitched. "So I'd be a guinea pig?"

That was too much! "I may not be a pro, but I *have* cut hair before, Josh. I used to do my friends in Springfield. One guy I dated was what you might call a cheapskate—"

Josh's rueful laugh interrupted her. "Maybe I'd better go to the barber shop. I don't mind paying for a haircut!"

"I know," she said quickly, not intending to get into another argument about what he could and could not afford. She'd learned her lesson about that. "But I'm pretty good. I promise, you wouldn't have to go around with a bag over your head to hide a bad haircut."

"I wouldn't know if you gave me a bad haircut or not." He was still smiling. "For that matter, I've probably had my share of bad haircuts, and not once did I wear a bag over my head."

"So what do you have to lose? You might as well let me trim it a little."

"Yes, well, I'm not sure where Mildred kept any decent scissors. I imagine they're someplace where the kids won't find them, which means I'm not likely to stumble across them, either."

"No problem. My good scissors were in one of my suitcases." Kath and Dina had come through like troopers and shipped Lily Ann's stuff to her; when she checked with the bus station on Wednesday, the luggage and boxes had just arrived, and it had taken the Lincoln to haul everything home. She hadn't yet unpacked it all.

Still not looking entirely convinced that this was a smart idea, he finally shrugged. "I don't know why you're asking for extra work, but I guess I shouldn't complain." He added in a resigned tone, "Anyway, it'll grow back."

Josh sat in the lawn chair that Lily Ann had situated near the back doorstep so she could keep an eye on the kids while she trimmed. He had a towel draped around his neck and an apprehensive feeling in his gut. After the way his nerves had reacted when she merely brushed the sand out of his hair, he wasn't sure he could bear up under a haircut. He regretted having brailled her face the other day. Knowing what she looked like only made things worse.

When Lily Ann started combing and snipping, Sarah propped her elbows on Josh's bare knees to observe the process in fascination. Samuel only watched for a minute before deciding that he'd better go dig a moat around the sand castle.

"Are you getting a haircut because it's church tomorrow, Uncle Josh?" Sarah asked.

He grunted at the reminder. Maybe he should have declined Lily Ann's offer, after all. There was no telling what shape his hair would be in when she got through.

But Lily Ann spoke up for him brightly. "Of course he is! You always like to look your best when you go to church, don't you?"

"I save my best clothes for Sunday," the little girl said. "Are you going with us, Lily Ann?"

Josh listened alertly to her answer. "I don't know. I hadn't thought that far ahead. Am I invited?"

"Sure! She can come, can't she, Uncle Josh? She could even drive the car, so Mrs. Newland wouldn't have to pick us up."

"Sarah," he said sharply, "Lily Ann might want some time to herself on Sunday. We don't want her to feel that she has to drive us, when several others have offered to give us a ride."

"Then again," Lily Ann put in, "maybe I'd actually *like* to go to church with you."

Getting the feeling she was amused at his expense, he said nothing more, although Sarah chattered at length about her Sunday schoolteacher and the children in her class.

When Sarah finally went off to join Samuel, the discussion of what Lily Ann would do the next day fizzled. She seemed to be concentrating on his hair, weaving her fingers in as she cut expertly, confidently. Yet there was a cautious quality to the movement of her hands, as if her fingertips were getting to know his hair, and his skin, very carefully indeed.

When she began gently massaging his scalp, he slid lower in the chair as a pure liquid heat flowed through him. Closing his eyes, he shivered and thought with a gulp that he'd never had a haircut quite like this one. He'd never realized a haircut could be an unforgettably sensual experience.

Her fingers stroked, slowed, then grew still. "You have a scar here, just inside your hairline."

"Only one? Are you sure?" His words came out muffled and drowsy. "My head tried to go through the windshield."

After a few moments of her silence, he realized the stillness had gripped her arms—possibly her whole body. When she finally spoke, her voice was hushed. "Was that when..."

"Yes." Stirred out of his absorption with the pleasurable weight of her hands, he sat up straighter. He frowned, wondering what on earth had prompted him to mention his accident. But he *had* mentioned it, and there was no point in blaming Lily Ann. "I was in a car wreck. It happened four years ago last October, while I was driving back to Colorado from a visit here."

Four years ago? *Coincidence*! she told herself, her heart protesting wildly.

She'd started trembling. Josh felt it just before she snatched back her hands from his not-quite-finished haircut. His lips tightened, and he drew a deep, frustrated breath. Her reaction was exactly why he didn't like to talk about the accident! That plus the fact that he didn't particularly relish the memories.

And then, to his astonishment, she pursued it. "Where did it happen?" she asked hoarsely.

"Does it matter?"

"Please, Josh." She sounded strained, and the hand that squeezed his shoulder was cool, almost icy.

The pressure was an apology and an appeal at the same time, and Josh gave in with a sigh. "It was in Kansas. In Wichita." Hearing her soft exclamation of dismay, he reached up absently to rub his eyes. "If I'd stayed on the Interstate instead of getting off to eat, the other guy wouldn't have hit my car."

She made a sound that he hoped wasn't a sob. But then in that same strangled voice she managed to ask, "Was he ... had he been drinking?"

"Isn't that usually the case? He'd started celebrating Halloween early—like three weeks early. Evidently his normal state was somewhere between plastered and smashed."

It was Pop. The thought filled her head, filled her entire being with despair, even as she tried to convince herself this didn't prove anything. She knew. It *was* Ned. She didn't have to ask Josh to confirm who had blinded him. She didn't dare ask, in fact. *Oh, dear God, please don't let him suspect!* What would Josh do if he ever found out Ned was her father?

She never knew how she managed to finish cutting Josh's hair. It was one of the hardest things she'd ever done, burdened down as she was by her guilty secret. Tears kept blinding her, so when she finally took away the towel from his neck and shook it, she couldn't really tell how he looked.

Sarah had no such problem. "Great job, Lily Ann!" she said, her head cocked to one side as she surveyed her uncle with approval written all over her small face.

Josh used both hands to smooth back his hair, then thanked Lily Ann in a distant, even voice.

After bath time, when the children were telling her goodnight, Sarah surprised Lily Ann by clinging to her hand. "Will you go with us in the morning?" the little girl asked. "Please?"

As she stood in confused misery, Lily Ann watched Josh kneel and put his arms around his niece. "I think Lily Ann has other plans, honey. Maybe she can go another time."

The only plans she had were to lock herself in her room and cry her eyes out. But Josh clearly thought her nearly total silence for the past hour somehow reflected on him. And no matter how difficult it was to look at him and not want to die inside for shame of her father, she couldn't let him go on thinking that.

She touched Sarah's curly hair, and the child raised eyes full of disappointment. "Wake me if I oversleep tomorrow, okay, sweetie? It'll take me a while to get ready for church."

"Okay!" Sarah gave Lily Ann a delighted hug before bouncing off to bed.

Josh went, too, looking as if he were restraining himself from saying something.

Chapter Eight

The yard had begun to resemble a jungle. Lily Ann scanned the scene from the front porch, shaking her head over the weed-infested flower beds and the distinctly untidy lawn of St. Augustine grass. She knew the backyard looked every bit as neglected as this. She also knew Josh would disapprove if he could see it.

A week of heavy rains early in May—besides leaving the kids hyper and deepening Lily Ann's melancholy—had greened all the plant life for miles around Bartlesville. The days of sunshine that followed had triggered a wild growth spurt, at the same time bringing some measure of healing to Lily Ann.

She still felt wretched, knowing what her own father had done, but at least she could function. She had come to a gradual understanding that if she tried to escape from reality by holing up in her room, it would only result in more problems for everyone.

Holing up had never been her style, anyway. Working till she dropped from exhaustion was more like it.

As she surveyed the overgrown grounds, she made up her mind. Josh had said not to worry about it—that Herman Farrell would do the yard work as soon as he could spare the time from his own farm. But this was ridiculous. The place was starting to look as if nobody lived here. There was no reason, no reason on earth, that she shouldn't get out the lawnmower and tackle the job.

Three hours later, tired, sweaty and highly pleased with the results of her labor, she pulled off the gardening gloves and hung the trimming shears back on the garage wall, wiped her feet, then entered the house through the utility room.

Josh and the children were sitting at the kitchen table, eating peanut-butter-and-banana sandwiches. Samuel grinned at her. "We thought you were never gonna come in."

"If you're hungry," Sarah added, "Uncle Josh will fix your lunch. He makes *scrunch-us* sandwiches."

With some difficulty she managed not to laugh. "They do look scrumptious, Miss Sarah. But I'd better clean up before I eat. I can fix myself something when I finish."

"All the bananas may be gone by then," Samuel warned her with an impish giggle.

She ruffled the little boy's hair in passing. "Then I'll just have to go to the store and buy some more, won't I, Samuel, my love?" He nodded complacently.

As she showered and dressed in shorts and a blouse, she reflected on how secure both children were . . . how confident of Josh's love. They trusted that they would be fed, clothed and sheltered no matter what. Having craved that kind of stability when she was young, she rejoiced to see it in these youngsters who had lost so much.

Evidently even Josh had begun to trust that Lily Ann would make good on her promise to stay. It had been at least a week since he'd exhibited signs of relief when she returned home from an errand. About time, too! she thought.

By the time she finally padded on bare feet back to the kitchen, the kids had settled down for their afternoon naps, and Josh had put together one of his "scrunch-us" peanut-butter-and-banana treats for her.

She was surprised and touched that he'd gone to the trouble. "Thanks," she said as she sat down in her usual place, her chair at right angles to his. "This looks good!"

"Does it? It feels gooey." He licked one finger absently.

She'd expected him to jump on her case about mowing the yard, but he didn't say much of anything while she was eating. *What the heck*, she thought. This might be the perfect time to bring up that other...

She cleared off the table first, then sat back down. "Uh, Josh—Sarah has mentioned a couple of times that she'd like to go on a picnic. Apparently they've talked lately in Sunday school about families going to the zoo and stuff like that. You know, fun things for kids." Lily Ann searched his face. "What do you think?"

He considered it, then shrugged one shoulder. "Mildred used to take the kids swimming and picnicking. I don't guess there's any reason why you shouldn't, if you don't mind."

"Me?" She frowned. "Sarah wants *you* to take them. Of course, I'll go, too, but—"

He was shaking his head. "I don't think so. It would be too much work."

Astonishment made her stare. This didn't sound like Josh at all! "Since when have you objected to working hard if it'll benefit Sarah and Samuel?"

Sliding his chair back from the table, he made an impatient gesture with one hand. "I'm talking about hard work for you, Lily Ann, not me! I'm not much good on picnics. I tend to slow everyone down. You'll have more fun if you and the kids go off by yourselves for the day."

Lily Ann's throat ached suddenly, sharply, and her heart protested. More fun? They couldn't have fun without him! But instinctively she kept her true feelings to herself, assuming a wryly amused tone. "Try telling Sarah that. Her mind is made up. A picnic's not a picnic without Uncle Josh."

"Sarah needs to learn that she won't always get what she wants in life," he said with irony equal to hers.

Dropping all pretense, Lily Ann made another appeal. "I think that's a lesson Sarah has already learned very well. And when you get right down to it, she doesn't ask for very much, does she?"

He muttered something beneath his breath about low blows, then clamped his lips shut and sighed. "I want to go on record. I may go along with your harebrained picnic idea, but I don't approve."

"Why not?"

"Because you've got enough to do without volunteering for more responsibilities. But that hasn't stopped you yet, has it? You gave me a haircut that earns me compliments every time I leave the house. You started going to church with us just to make the kids happy. You insist on doing my yard work even though I pay someone else to do it. You've organized every room in the house—just about every aspect of our lives. Isn't that enough for you?"

Lily Ann had grown very still. "You're not happy with my work?"

Standing, Josh made his way around the table and over to the cabinet. As if to prove the point of what he'd just said about her organizational talents, he quickly got down two glasses and began filling them with ice from the dispenser on the refrigerator door, then with freshly brewed tea from a pitcher on the counter. He carried them back to the table and, with almost a flourish, set one before Lily Ann. Then he sat down again with his own drink and turned a calm smile in her direction.

"How could I not be happy with your work?" he asked pointedly. "Your job performance isn't the problem here."

"What *is* the problem, then?" She felt bewildered and worried. If the solution wasn't to work a little harder, she was afraid she wouldn't be able to correct whatever was wrong.

"The problem," he said slowly, as if trying to decide how to put it, "is your... your obsession with being the perfect housekeeper. I don't expect perfection from you, Lily Ann. I don't even *want* it. Perfect people are hard to be around."

"I'm not perfect," she said in a small voice. *Oh, Lord, Josh, if you only knew!*

"Aren't you?" He rubbed his jaw a minute, thinking hard. "What is it about being here that scares you?" he finally asked.

"*Scares* me? What makes you think... I'm not scared!"

"Well, something's threatening you. You're trying too hard to get control of things." He didn't look thrilled at having to say this, but he continued anyway. "That's why you insist on neatness and organization. It's your way of attempting to control your life."

His matter-of-fact words might have come from a case study in a textbook. She remembered when she was straightening a closet and found his framed college diploma on a shelf, along with a certificate showing that he'd passed his state licensing exam as a psychological associate. No wonder the novels he wrote had such an edge—such a tendency to grab hold of the emotions and not let go!

And now it would seem that from time to time he drew upon his knowledge in order to analyze his employees! The thing that really disturbed Lily Ann was that he was correct in his assessment of her. She *did* want to gain control.

Shaken, she said, "I thought you liked organization. I thought a neat environment was a plus for you."

"It is." He hesitated, one hand circling the iced tea glass and drawing it closer. But rather than take a drink, he sat tracing the beaded rim with the tip of his index finger. Finally he raised his head. "I apologize, Lily Ann. Obviously I've hurt your feelings, and that wasn't my intention." His expression was intent, as if he wished more than anything that he could meet her eyes, make her listen to him. "I don't want you to take on too much around here and burn yourself out. Sarah and Samuel need you—not just for one picnic, but every day." He forced a rather lopsided smile. "You wouldn't be easy to replace, you know."

"I'm not going to burn out." Her voice wasn't quite steady. "I can handle this picnic, Josh." Something made her add, "So can you."

His smile grew even more crooked, but he didn't argue.

Lily Ann drove the Lincoln along the rutted lane that edged the wheat field, parking it near the beginning of the copse of trees. When she got out, she could see a creek meandering through the trees with shady green banks that would make an idyllic setting for a picnic.

"You were right. It *is* perfect," she told Josh when he climbed out, too.

He remembered the spot, located in the middle of his family's farm, from fishing expeditions when he was a youth. He'd worn a fondly reminiscent smile as he told her about the deep clear pool where he and his brother and their friends had gone swimming.

While he helped the kids out of the back seat, she unlocked the trunk and took out two large shopping bags containing the food. "One for each of you to carry," she informed Sarah and Samuel, placing the bags in their hands. "Not too heavy, are they?" Both enthusiastically shook their heads.

"This is your burden." She pressed a folded quilt against Josh's chest, and he obediently closed his arms around it, his expression quizzical. "Before you accuse me of forgetting your cane, let me tell you that you won't need it. You can hold the blanket with one arm and hold on to me with the other."

"Sounds as if you've got it all figured out," he drawled, shifting the quilt into the crook of his left arm. His face enigmatic, he waited for her to shut the trunk and stuff the car keys into the pocket of her jeans.

"I certainly tried." She picked up the small ice chest with her right hand and moved closer to him. "Ready?"

Josh found her left arm and wrapped his fingers around it firmly. "As ready as I'll ever be."

They started out, Lily Ann half a step ahead of Josh, Sarah and Samuel bringing up the rear. After a short distance, though, Josh halted, scowling. "Are you carrying something heavy?"

"Just the cooler, but it's not really very—"

"Here. Let me have it." He interrupted her curtly, reached out to take the handle of the ice chest from her, then transferred the quilt into her arms. "I can feel you being pulled off balance."

She clutched the quilt, her face warm. "Sorry."

He shrugged. "Let's try again."

This time they made it all the way to the creek bank and soon had lunch laid out in the middle of the blanket, under a sprawling oak. Lily Ann had packed ham sandwiches, fried chicken, dill pickles, cherry tomatoes, oat-raisin muffins, apples and cheese slices—all finger foods that Josh could manage easily. And as usual, she'd gone overboard, bringing more than the four of them could possibly consume at one sitting.

When Sarah asked the blessing, her words brought a smile to Lily Ann's face. "Dear Father, thank you for making this picnic come true," Sarah prayed. "Maybe we can come back tomorrow."

After they'd finished eating, Lily Ann repacked the shopping bags and set them in the fork of a nearby tree, out of reach of varmints. When she turned back, she discovered that Josh had stretched out flat on his back along one side of the big blanket, with a drowsy Samuel tucked in close to him and Sarah next to Sam.

Yawning, the little girl patted the quilt beside her. "Here's a place for you, Lily Ann. It's nap time."

Something twisted Lily Ann's heart as she lay down on her side, facing the other three. This was what a family looked like! And it hurt, knowing she wasn't really a part of their family.

Don't think about that, she told herself. *Why not play like you're really part of it....*

With her head resting on one arm, she lay watching the others. The dark-haired, angel-faced children were already drifting off, lulled to dreamland by the heat of the May afternoon, the chirping birds and the breeze sighing through the branches overhead. Josh's eyes were closed, too, the long lashes fanning his sculpted cheekbones, his mouth relaxed.

It was a sexy mouth. Funny that she'd never labeled it that before. She had an urge to kiss it now, and she pretended for a few minutes that he was her husband—that Sarah and Samuel belonged to both of them. While the kids slept, she could get up and circle the blanket and kneel down to touch her lips to his. She already knew how delicious he tasted....

Stirred by the vividness of her fantasy, Lily Ann felt a pleasant warmth steal through her veins, melting her with the desire to kiss Josh again. A real kiss, like that time after her first visit to the bank.

She watched him from beneath lowered lashes, studying his long, tightly muscled shape in his faded jeans and polo shirt. When he kissed her, he'd enfolded her in his powerful arms and molded her to his body, and it had felt wonderful! She'd never felt so incredibly alive, nor so beautiful, because he told her she was.

Oh, Lord, please don't ever let him stop thinking that of me! she prayed, her breath catching in her chest. *Don't let him ever come to hate me because of something I couldn't help!*

A shudder coursed through her. She forced herself to stop pretending they were a family and tried to be content with knowing she was doing the very best she could to smooth over the difficulties of his life. It would have to be enough.

After a sleepy hour and then a bit of barefoot splashing in the creek, they put on shoes and socks again and started back to where the car was parked. Lily Ann was enjoying the walk, the quiet feeling of closeness to Josh as he held her arm, the happy laughter of the children.

She turned her head and looked over her shoulder to make sure the kids weren't trailing too far behind, and before she could face the front again, Josh caught his foot on a half-buried stone. It sent him plunging forward, the ice chest flying in another direction.

"Josh!" She dropped to her knees beside him, afraid he might be hurt. "Oh, Josh, I'm sorry!"

His mouth was grim, but he looked uninjured as he got back to his feet. When she began to brush the dirt and twigs from his clothes, he pushed her away. "I'll do it."

She apologized again as he was getting into the car, and he snapped at her. "It wasn't your fault. These things happen." Turning his head away, he added, "I told you I'm no good on picnics. Next time maybe you'll listen."

Chapter Nine

The words were no sooner out of his mouth than Josh regretted them. He shouldn't have lashed out at Lily Ann. As he'd said, it wasn't her fault. The problem was that he hated appearing clumsy in front of her. After nearly five years, he still wasn't reconciled to the sheer frustrating inconvenience of being blind, and he didn't know if he ever would be.

He couldn't apologize, though. Pride wouldn't let him, even when he thought about what it would be like never to go on another picnic with Lily Ann and the children. Never again to anticipate the seductive feel of her fingers lacing into his hair as she gave him a trim. Never again to have her sit up late with him in the living room while they listened to the classical FM radio station, or stay at his side in church, where in spite of some very caring friends he sometimes felt lonely and out of place, as if he and Sarah and Samuel were merely the shattered remains of a family.

Barren, bleak, boring—several words came to mind to describe his days before Lily Ann had started brightening them with her lively companionship, her silky voice and her fragrant warmth that he occasionally got to reach out and touch. Following her suggestions might mean risking a few undignified tumbles, but that sure beat the alternative of sitting at home while she and the kids went places without him.

Even so, he didn't apologize. Instead he spent the rest of the day, and most of the next, in a blue funk, calling himself a fool because he couldn't force out the words that he knew he ought to say.

That evening after supper, Lily Ann escorted Sarah and Samuel into the study where Josh sat with a mystery novel on the desk in front of him. He'd lost track of the time, although not because he was engrossed in the plot; in fact, he couldn't remember turning a page since he opened the book.

"I promised the kids if they were good today, we could go to town and get an ice cream." She sounded briskly determined. "We'd like you to come with us."

Josh lifted his head and kept his fingertips in place as if he'd been reading. Feeling a surge of intense pleasure, he tried to school his face not to show his relief.

Her breathing suspended, Lily Ann waited to see how Josh would react. Ever since yesterday she had wanted to wrap him tightly in her arms and promise him she would never again be so careless as to let him stumble and fall— that she would rather cut off her right arm than ever see him hurt. But that would have revealed a degree of caring that was inappropriate for a housekeeper. He must never know the way she was starting to feel about him . . . nor must he ever guess that even if she had cared nothing for him personally, she would still give him her faithful service because of what Ned Jones had done to him.

All other logic aside, something told Lily Ann to ignore his sulky outburst and his subsequent moodiness and just act as if nothing had happened. If she made a big deal of the way he'd fallen, she would be validating it as a tragedy.

Josh closed the book slowly, his face still inscrutable. Then he stood up and slid his hand across the desk to find his folded cane.

"Ice cream sounds good." He congratulated himself on his convincing show of nonchalance.

As they drove the two miles toward Bartlesville, the gathering darkness settled over the countryside, while lights blinked on all around them like glittering jewels. Twilight was, in Lily Ann's opinion, the nicest time of day, and a spring evening like this was one for the books. For a sharply poignant moment, she wanted to tell Josh how peaceful and lovely everything looked. Then he lowered his window and savored a long, deep breath of the fresh air, and she realized he must be enjoying his own pleasant version of their surroundings.

Being in town after dark had set off Sarah's bubbling excitement. "We're getting to stay up late, aren't we?"

"Later than you usually do," Lily Ann agreed, pulling the car into the crowded parking lot at the ice-cream store and finding only one free space at the rear. Evidently this was everyone's favorite place to gather.

Josh opened the crystal of his braille watch and felt the hands, his expression registering faint surprise as he discovered the time.

"We're lucky!" Samuel said.

"You sure are!" Josh muttered dryly.

"Well, lucky or not, we wouldn't be getting ice cream if you weren't such good kids," Lily Ann praised them as she opened her car door.

Josh used his cane to cross the parking lot, but just outside the door of the restaurant Lily Ann murmured a warning about the madhouse inside. "You might want to hang on to my arm. If we get separated, one of us could be lost in the mob and never heard from again."

The mocking grin that tugged at Josh's lips told her he knew which one was likely to get lost, but he merely folded his cane and took her arm. As if he'd waved a magic wand, the instant his fingers touched her bare skin they liberated a swarm of high-strung butterflies in her stomach, making her shiver.

"Hey, Delaney!"

"Good grief, would you look who just came in! It's Bartlesville's answer to Poe."

"Good to see you, man!"

"About time you brought Sarah and Samuel in here, Josh. What d'you say, kids? You got a hug for me?"

The greetings drifted over to them from all sides. Even more conscious than before of Josh's firm grip on her arm, Lily Ann smiled cautiously at those who spoke and left it to him to reply, except when she saw someone she knew, like Bill Akin. Josh seemed to recognize all the voices and responded amiably. In between shaking hands and returning an embrace from one or two demonstrative female friends, he always made sure Lily Ann was safely within reach and resumed his hold on her as quickly as he could.

Once they got their order, they joined Paul and Kim Newland at a corner booth. It seemed that the Newlands, who lived just a bit farther out of town than Josh and belonged to the same church, had only been married a year but had dated since Kim was seventeen. By listening quietly, Lily Ann figured out that Paul had been a couple of years behind Josh in high school, where both had played on the varsity basketball team. She also learned that the ruggedly built Paul was a farmer while Kim had given up a promising modeling career in Dallas to return to her hometown and teach kindergarten.

It was clear to Lily Ann that the stunning redhead loved children almost as much as she adored her gentle, plain-featured husband and wanted to have his child as soon as they decided they could afford it. "If you and Josh would like to go out some evening," Kim said as they were all walking out to their cars together, "we'll be glad for Sarah and Samuel to stay with us." Paul echoed the invitation with warmth and genuine enthusiasm.

Lily Ann wasn't sure how to respond. She didn't think it was her place to point out that she was Josh's employee, not his girlfriend. Josh had always been flexible about her job description, but she was fairly sure that dating the boss wasn't included in either her duties or her privileges. To her discomfort, she had to admit that dating the boss was just the beginning of what she wanted to do with him.

Josh thanked the Newlands for the offer and let it go at that, aware that the suggestion had made Lily Ann withdraw even further into a watchful mood. She obviously didn't want to have to deal with the possibility of spending time with him alone. It was one thing to accompany him and his niece and nephew on a picnic or to get an ice-cream cone. Going somewhere with him on a one-to-one basis was something else again, and he could see why the idea wouldn't exactly thrill her.

* * *

The ice-cream outing had been fun, Lily Ann thought the next day as she sat on the front porch, a yellow legal pad on her lap and pen in hand. But it was just one more aspect of her new job that she'd better not mention in her letter to Kathleen and Dina. She had to be careful not to let her growing attachment to Josh become evident to *anyone*. She could only hope her feelings hadn't been too obvious to Kim and Paul. That could account for their offer to baby-sit the kids ...

Banishing the thought, she finished the closing paragraph: "As soon as I can arrange a day off, I'll drive to Springfield and get my things out of your way. I'm enclosing a check to cover what it cost you to send my clothes, with a little something extra for your trouble. Don't argue with me on this—just go out to eat, okay?" She signed, folded and stuffed it and the check into an envelope that she'd already addressed, and hurried out to the mailbox just as the van driven by the rural mail carrier appeared. The letter satisfied her, since she hadn't given away any secrets in it.

After chatting a moment with the mailman, Lily Ann went back to the house with the handful of mail that had come for Josh. Seeing that the children were playing school in the front hall, she headed for Josh's study, where he was sitting with his feet propped up on the desk, listening to a Talking Book through headphones.

She tapped his wrist to get his attention, and he quickly shut off the cassette player and swung his feet down. Removing the headphones, he automatically ran his fingers through his hair to smooth it. "What is it, Lily Ann?"

She no longer found it quite so odd that he shouldn't need to ask who had interrupted him. There were several clues—the fact that her touch was much more restrained than either of the children's would have been, for instance. And then there was her scent, which she hadn't even known she possessed, but which Josh assured her was quite distinctive, even when she wore no perfume. She fervently hoped that he considered her fragrance attractive.

"Mail call." She opened his briefcase where it lay on a bookshelf. "The telephone and electric bills came, so I'm putting them in your briefcase so we can take them to Grover. There's also a coupon for pizza and a sweepstakes entry from some publishing company."

"Trash 'em."

"Done!" She dropped the two items into the wastebasket, as always gaining a sense of accomplishment when she got rid of junk mail. "And last but not least, there's an airmail letter with foreign postage on it. It's from a K. Wright whose return address is...uh, it looks like Calcutta."

"Kael!" Josh leaned forward, looking so pleased that his eyes seemed to light up. "He's in India now, hmm? What does he say?"

Lily Ann read him the letter, struggling over scrawled, nearly illegible words of apology for going so long since last writing. "'But it's not as if you ever write me back, buddy,'" the man scolded him. "'Couldn't you at least ask good ol' Mildred to drop me a line like you used to do and let me know what's happening in your part of the world?'"

She stopped reading at that point and gave Josh a searching look. As if he sensed her scrutiny, he shrugged, his expression somber. "I haven't had a chance to let Kael know Mildred died. He moves around a lot, so I don't have a telephone number for him, and it's been, I don't know, at least three months since he called here. He's right in the middle of doing some research and may not be back home in Denver until late in the year."

In those terrible days right after they lost Mildred, and then again when he began to suspect Rena couldn't be trusted, Josh would have given anything to be able to contact his best friend and ask him to fly back to the States, to Bartlesville. Kael wouldn't have hesitated to come if he'd had any idea his help was needed. But he, too, had believed Josh's longtime housekeeper was immortal.

Lily Ann resumed reading the letter aloud, describing the research Kael was doing in the prisons of India—research that he planned to use in a book comparing the criminal justice systems of various countries. "'But enough about my idea of fun. I want to know about Baxter Monroe. How's the fella coming along? Any juicy idiosyncrasies developing that you'd care to share with a friend?'"

She paused again to ask, "Baxter Monroe?"

His face rueful, Josh rested his chin on the palm of his hand, his elbow on the desk. "Just a character I made the mistake of mentioning to Kael the last time he was here."

"A character?"

"A fictional character." When Lily Ann kept waiting, Josh sighed and shifted to lean back in the chair. He looked uncomfortable talking about this. "Sometimes people begin to inhabit my mind. People that have a story to tell. After a while they begin to be very real...as real as some folks I've known all my life."

"That sounds interesting but...distracting," she said.

"It's one of the hazards of being a writer, and as you know, I used to be one of those."

"So...is Baxter in residence?"

He smiled rather bleakly. "From time to time. I try to ignore him, hoping he'll go away."

"But he has a story to tell?" she asked quietly.

When he just shrugged, she thought a moment. Finally she asked, "Why don't you tell his story, then?"

Josh looked undecided whether to be angry or amused. "How am I supposed to do that?"

"How did you used to do it?"

"On the computer."

She considered it some more before confiding, "You know, I'm pretty good with a word processing program."

"Well, bully for you!"

That caused Lily Ann to smile gently, remembering how she'd tried to taunt him out of a grouchy mood the first night she arrived here. "Yes, Josh. Bully for me." Eyeing his disk drive and monitor, she added, "If you dictate Baxter's story to me, I'll put it on the computer."

"In your spare time?" he asked with noticeable sarcasm.

"I could let Mr. Farrell do the yard. And what the heck—I don't guess I have to wash the windows *every* week. Come on, Josh, let's at least give it a shot."

"It would never work. You have too much to do."

"I think you're afraid to try."

"Yeah, well, sometimes I think you're just plain crazy."

Lily Ann sat in Josh's chair, her hands on the computer keyboard, her smile satisfied. Josh was sprawled on the sofa, looking as if he was wondering how he'd got there.

But Josh knew just how it had happened: He'd been unable to resist. The thought of actually writing again had lured him straight into Lily Ann's web. So what if he was worried that his talent might have rusted beyond redemption from years of not being used? Wasn't it Samuel Johnson who'd said that nothing would ever be attempted if all possible objections had to be overcome first?

Steeling himself to meet the test, Josh had stopped objecting and had agreed that they should work together on Baxter's story as soon as they had some quiet time. The kids had gone to bed at eight o'clock and now, three hours later, Josh was five pages into the first chapter. A remarkable accomplishment, all things considered. And it had sounded pretty good when Lily Ann read it back to him. Maybe there was hope.

Two weeks later he was ready to concede that point: There was *definitely* hope. He and Lily Ann had formed the habit of writing every evening, as well as during the children's nap times on days when they could persuade them to take naps. But ever since the picnic, Sarah and Samuel had pleaded more and more often for Josh to accompany them on outings, and he had found himself more and more agreeable.

They spent almost an entire day at the nearby Woolaroc Wildlife Preserve and Museum, a 3,600-acre park that offered a nature trail and numerous educational exhibits, plus picnic facilities where they had lunch. Lily Ann promised the children they could go back once the petting zoo opened for the summer; in the meantime, they saw zebras, buffalo, elk, ostriches, mustangs, longhorn cattle and several kinds of deer as they drove through the preserve. It was enough excitement to keep the kids talking for days.

Then, driving just five miles north of Bartlesville, they toured a museum full of memorabilia from Tom Mix, a legendary movie star known as the "King of the Cowboys." And on yet another day they visited a modern buffalo ranch, learning all about the buffalo industry as a guide took them for a ride on a tractor-drawn wagon.

To his surprise, Josh found that he enjoyed these outings as much as the others did. These were places he'd wanted to share with Sarah and Sam—places he'd loved from his own youth and had never thought he would be able to take them. But what he'd really never guessed was how much fun it would be with Lily Ann beside him. She had a way of slipping her hand into his that erased all his worry about stumbling, at the same time making him ache inside with a sweetly painful hunger. Not only that, but she never seemed to mind his dependence on her in unfamiliar places. And she smelled too good to believe.

Josh sank into the desk chair that Lily Ann usually occupied these days and extended his hand to pat the neat stack of manuscript pages she had printed out. Five chapters. More than enough to send in to Phil McKay and get his opinion as an editor. Lily Ann was encouraging him to go for it, the way she encouraged him in everything. Lord, what had he ever done before she came along?

And why was she so much braver on his behalf than she was on her own? Her faith in him seemed limitless; she believed he could do anything and thought he ought to try—at least that was the impression she gave. But when it came to tooting her own horn, she clammed up. He'd never met anyone with so many varied talents and such . . . such drive and dedication.

Yet she seemed to feel it was only through her hard work that she had earned a place here. She seemed not even to realize how much the kids adored her, and how much Josh had come to appreciate her just for herself, although perhaps it was just as well if she didn't know that.

What if she had plans to move on? What would he do when she left? After all, he couldn't be sure she would stay. She never talked about Lily Ann Jones; Josh still knew little about her before she came to Bartlesville and even less about how she felt about things right now.

The jangling telephone broke into his contemplation of the mystery, and he answered it on the first ring. His mood plummeted when he recognized Betty Ludlow's voice. Ever since her first visit soon after Mildred died he'd done his best to discourage the social worker from coming back. Thankfully she hadn't called in weeks, but he couldn't put her off forever.

Lily Ann didn't mean to eavesdrop; she had just come in search of Josh to ask his preference for supper when the phone rang and he answered it. As she waited in the doorway, she realized he was speaking in a voice so stiff and wary it was almost unrecognizable. "Everything's going okay. I haven't contacted your office because we've had no problems. There was no reason to bother you."

She began to feel anxious. Who was he talking to?

"Tomorrow?" He reached up to massage his forehead. "I'm afraid we won't be home then, but I could leave the key if you want to inspect the house—" He broke off, his jaw tensing. "I want you to see for yourself that my housekeeper is doing an outstanding job of cleaning the place. She's a good cook, and the children love her, too."

His words transfixed Lily Ann. What on earth!

"Look, Mrs. Ludlow—" Josh was starting to sound a bit desperate "—I know what you thought the last time you were here, but that was nearly two months ago. The situation turned around completely after that, and we're getting along fine now." As he listened to the woman on the other end, he clenched his jaw until the muscles bunched up. "If somebody has an accident, I can dial the telephone and get help. For that matter, the housekeeper is capable of driving us to the hospital. She's a safe driver.... My banker checked her out." He paused, then snapped, "Excuse me, Mrs. Ludlow, but I have to go now.

If you'd like to make a home visit, why don't you call back next week for an appointment? In the meantime, you'll just have to take my word for it that things have never been better here.''

Chapter Ten

Josh hung up the phone and turned toward the doorway. "Lily Ann?" With that alert, well-developed perception of his, he knew she was there. "You've mentioned that you need to go to Springfield to take care of some things. I guess I ought to insist that you take off as long as you need and go, but... what would you say to the four of us driving up there tomorrow? We could come back on Sunday, or even later if we're enjoying it."

Lily Ann studied his dark, attractive features, the smoke-gray eyes half-closed, the sexy mouth bracketed with lines of tension. Tension over what? Certainly not a sudden, passionate desire to go sightseeing in Missouri. No, it was more likely a pressing neend to get away from something or someone. Someone like Mrs. Ludlow, the social worker that he was worried would try to take Sarah and Samuel away from him.

Every time Josh had suggested that she needed some time off, Lily Ann had refused. What she had never told him, and couldn't tell him now, was that she simply didn't want to be somewhere that he wasn't. Time off held no appeal for her. "If you want to go to Springfield, Josh, I'm ready."

Relaxing visibly, he nodded.

They got everything packed that afternoon and then left in the Lincoln at midmorning the next day after a leisurely breakfast and a trip to the post office to mail Josh's manuscript. Normally it would have been a three-and-a-half-hour drive to Springfield, but Lily Ann stretched it out with frequent stops for the kids and time out for a picnic lunch at a rest area on the Interstate. Thinking ahead, she had brought along some sandwiches rather than subject Josh to a meal in a restaurant. He hated to eat out, being convinced that his occasionally awkward table manners would embarrass whoever was with him. Every chance she got, she tried to persuade him that he was too hard on himself, but he still wouldn't undertake anything more complicated than an ice-cream cone in public.

They reached the southwestern Missouri city with time to spare before rush-hour traffic, and Lily Ann pulled into one of the many motor hotels in the metropolitan area of over two hundred thousand residents. As she got out of the car to see about registering them, she wondered if this new-looking inn was going to prove expensive. She was glad her bank balance had grown sufficiently plump to survive the extravagance, because she refused to ask Josh and the children to stay somewhere that wasn't clean and safe and comfortable.

"Lily Ann." When Josh spoke her name, she leaned down to look in the open car door and saw that he was holding out a credit card to her. "Put the rooms on this."

For a minute she literally couldn't speak as she was struck by the significance of what Josh was doing. After the way Rena had tried to take advantage of him, he was giving Lily Ann permission to use his credit card! Either he was a fool, or he trusted her a great deal. And she knew Joshua Delaney was not a fool.

She cleared her throat. "Josh, that's not necessary. I'll pay for the rooms. We made the trip to Springfield to take care of my business, not yours."

"I asked you to come. I want to pay."

"How about if you pay for your room and I pay for mine?"

"How about if you stop giving me a hard time and just do as I say? I thought I was supposed to be the boss." His arm still extended, he waved the plastic in her general direction.

Lily Ann reluctantly took it. "Yes, *sir*!" she said with wry emphasis.

She was able to get them adjoining rooms on the ground floor. After they had unloaded the luggage from the car, she inspected Josh and Samuel's room, then guided Josh around while he learned its layout. "Here's the phone," she said, placing his hand on the receiver. "Just dial my room if you need me, and I can be here before you hang up."

He was standing close to her with her hand still covering his—so close she was trapped in his delicious male scent. She saw his lips part and his head tilt her way, a single line appearing between his eyebrows. Too late she realized that to have suggested he might need her could have sounded insulting or even...had it been provocative? Would he get the idea she was making advances toward him? Quickly she drew back her hand.

"I imagine Sam and I will be okay," he said evenly.

"Oh, well, sure. *Samuel* will be with you! Of course you'll be okay."

He smiled as though she had said something faintly amusing. "What's next on our agenda?"

She checked her watch. By now, unless they had dates, Kathleen and Dina had probably returned from work to the complex where they had neighboring apartments. "I guess I should call my friends and see when I can get my things."

"Okay." He found one of the easy chairs and sat down.

Pleased at the novel idea of staying in a motel, Sarah and Samuel were each testing a big bed, lying spread-eagle in the middle and pretending to be asleep. Lily Ann smiled to herself at their antics, stalling for time, not sure she wanted to make the call in front of Josh. But it would be rude to excuse herself and go to the room she was to share with Sarah, so she finally perched on the edge of one bed, picked up the telephone and dialed.

A minute passed before she hung up and dialed another number. "Hmph! Neither one answers. I guess we'd better make plans of our own this evening." She looked at Josh. "Any suggestions?"

Again he smiled that very slight smile. "This is your town, Lily Ann, not mine."

She pondered briefly. "Okay, we'll go to the zoo."

It was the perfect solution, she thought later as they sat on a tree-shaded bench near the center of the park. They were eating their supper—hot dogs bought from a vendor near the elephant exhibit. Even Josh had been forced to concede that a bit of fumbling wasn't going to matter here, and the kids were loving every minute of the experience.

Although she didn't tell Josh so, Lily Ann loved it, too, because exploring the zoo meant hands-on contact with him for hours at a time. By the time they returned to where they'd parked the car, she had begun to feel rather dreamy...something similar to the way being enchanted must feel. From the smiles of approval other people bestowed on them in passing, she knew they appeared to be a genuine family: a happily married couple with two small children who happened to bear a strong resemblance to their dark father. She had caught herself pretending that they were what they seemed, and she wished the fantasy didn't have to end—wished Josh would go on holding her arm, touching her, accidentally brushing against her as they walked side by side, then slipping his arm around her waist in silent apology.

Sometimes he left his arm there for a while—casually, as if distracted—and she really didn't think she could contain the joy swelling inside her when that happened. It was a joy that was sweeter yet more exquisitely painful, more fulfilling and at the same time more confusing, than any she'd ever known before. And she was afraid of what it meant. She was terrified that this was the joy of love.

Outside their motel rooms, Josh hugged and kissed Sarah as he told her good-night and Lily Ann did the same to Samuel. Before he went inside, however, the little boy mumbled sleepily, "Now your turn." Reaching up, he took his uncle's hand and guided it to Lily Ann's.

When Josh's fingers closed around hers, Lily Ann gazed up at him with such acute longing trembling through her that it was a wonder he didn't feel the powerful emotion behind her look. It took all her inner fortitude to make herself say lightly, "I think he wants you to kiss me good-night."

"So I gathered." Looking grave, Josh slid both arms around her and pulled her carefully against him. He rested his cheek on top of her silky hair, then pressed his lips to her forehead, and for a moment their hearts pounded together, chest to chest. Then his mouth brushed hers.

Never in her life had Lily Ann been as conscious of anything as she was the hard-muscled length of him and the warm strength and security of his embrace. She felt one of his hands stroke her back, and then he slowly dropped his arms.

"Good night, Lily Ann." His voice was husky.

"See you in the morning, Josh." Hers was a whisper.

She had difficulty falling asleep. For a long time she lay listening to Sarah's quiet breathing, thinking about the child's words as she tucked her into bed: "I wish you could be my mommy, Lily Ann. I have Uncle Josh, and I have Samuel, but I need a mommy." Lily Ann would have given anything to be the mother the little girl hungered for. It was obvious Sarah already felt she had a daddy in Josh.

Lily Ann thought about Josh then until, confronted with the no longer avoidable fact that she had fallen in love with him, she got up to pace the floor. Oh, dear Lord, what was she going to do about it? It wasn't as if they could have any kind of future together! She might yearn to spend the rest of her living days with that man—she might wish with all her heart that she were in the next room at this very moment, enfolded in his arms—but she had no reason to believe he would ever feel the same about her. And she couldn't even bear to think about how he would react if he found out Ned Jones was her father. That would kill any affection for her that might have started to grow. In fact, she wouldn't be surprised if it made Josh want to kill *her*—perhaps not literally, but in every other way!

The past few weeks of working on Josh's book had given her an uneasy insight into his attitude about revenge. Evidently he thought about the subject a lot. The main character in his story, Baxter Monroe, was a Southerner of aristocratic heritage. Once the object of envy and respect, he was alone now, disgraced and impoverished by

the loss of his wife and the collapse of his family's financial empire. Seeing no way out of his misery, Baxter considered himself doomed to end it all in a New Orleans
gutter. He just couldn't quite give up on life until he figured out how to drag down the man he blamed for his ruin.

The book made compelling reading. Lily Ann could already see evidence of Baxter's decline into madness as he
plotted against his enemy, and she finished each writing
session nearly breathless with fascination over what
scheme he'd cook up next. It was a kind of helpless fascination, because she feared Josh was writing about his own
hatred for Ned—feared it, but wasn't reckless enough to
ask him.

Her head aching, Lily Ann finally fell into bed and into
a troubled sleep. The next morning, although still anxious, she made up her mind to take things just one day at
a time. As long as Josh and the children needed a housekeeper, there was a chance their future would include her.

Tender pride stirred inside her when Josh suggested that
they breakfast in the motel restaurant. He ordered toast
and bacon to everyone else's pancakes and scrambled eggs,
but it represented progress. Apparently he was beginning
to realize the world didn't really care if he ate his bacon
with his fingers.

The visit to Kathleen's apartment—which Lily Ann had
both looked forward to and dreaded, in light of her chums'
curiosity—went fairly well. She called ahead right after
breakfast, so both Kath and Dina came outside with ex-
pectant faces to greet Lily Ann and the mysterious new
boss that they were sure they wouldn't like. It would have
been fun to capture their changing expressions on film as
they peered past her and got a good look at Josh. He
waited with the kids at the car, leaning against the front

fender, his small adorable charges doing their best to copy his relaxed pose.

Her friends were so overwhelmed by Josh's good looks, they didn't register much else until after they had helped her put her TV and the cartons of her other belongings in the spacious trunk of his car. Kathleen asked them to come inside, stressing how much news they had to catch up on. Only when Josh opened the watch on his sunbronzed wrist and fingered the dial, then agreed that they could spare some time for a visit—only then did it dawn on them why he hadn't budged more than a couple of steps from the car and why he'd worn a dark unsmiling look instead of helping the three women carry out the heavy boxes.

Watching Kath and Dina exchange startled glances, Lily Ann bristled and grew fiercely protective. She moved straight to Josh's side and waited for him to take her arm, then lifted her chin and met her friends' eyes. And instantly her defensiveness evaporated, because there was nothing but affection and warm understanding in the faces that looked back at her. They might not have any idea why she'd gone to work for Josh, but they didn't blame her a bit for staying.

For a while they all sat around the living room and talked, with Kathleen obviously itching to ask a hundred questions, and the more restrained Dina just managing to keep her from it with furtive elbow jabs and quelling frowns. After an hour of struggling to keep the conversation on safe ground, Lily Ann took the children's subdued fidgeting as a cue to make their excuses. She explained that they were on their way to tour the Wilson's Creek National Battlefield before driving the forty miles to Branson, otherwise known as the Country Music Capitol of the U.S.

Just before he climbed back into the Lincoln, Josh turned and reached out to shake hands with Dina, then Kathleen. "Until today I didn't realize how much Lily Ann must have missed you." He sounded regretful. "I've been selfish enough to make sure she knows we need her, otherwise I imagine she would've come back to see you before now. But maybe you can visit her sometime." His voice dropped a note, as if he were thinking aloud. "I hope so, anyway."

Lily Ann could see her friends eyeing Josh carefully, trying to figure out whether he meant the invitation. She wondered the same thing herself, although in her experience he wasn't prone to say things he didn't mean. His concern that she sustain the relationship with her best friends left her feeling more confused than ever about Josh.

She had plenty to think about as they drove back to Bartlesville on Tuesday afternoon. They'd extended their stay in Missouri because of Branson's many wholesome entertainment options designed for the entire family.

Besides taking in several music shows and an 1880s theme park called Silver Dollar City, they attended an evening performance of the "Shepherd Of The Hills" outdoor drama based on the legendary, action-packed book about the Ozarks at the turn of the century. The play's combination of mystery and romance enthralled Lily Ann while its exciting scenes of the good guys defeating the bad guys kept Sarah's and Samuel's eyes glued to the front of the amphitheater. Since Josh had read the book sometime in the past, he was able to follow the plot with the aid of some realistic sound effects and an occasional word from Lily Ann. At one of the saddest points near the end, when she was trying not to let anybody know she was crying, Josh wrapped an arm around her and gathered her close without saying anything, and love filled her heart so painfully full she really thought it might burst.

After that first night at the Springfield motel he gave her a good-night kiss every evening, and he didn't even wait to be prompted by Samuel, their determined little Cupid. His kisses—the incredibly vital feel of being in his arms, the clean taste of his mouth and the scent of his cologne, the heart-thudding, breathless, intoxicating effect on all her senses—branded themselves into her, body, soul and mind, so that it became almost impossible to stand it each time he drew back his arms and released her. The probability that even these too-brief kisses would cease once they were home again made her wish the trip would never end.

But it had to, of course. It was after three o'clock when they reached the farmhouse, and despite her fantasies, Lily Ann was glad to be there. It was home.

Everyone helped unload the car; even Josh insisted he could find his bedroom as easily with a suitcase in one hand as he could without. Lily Ann's possessions went into a storage cabinet in the garage, and after that the tired children traipsed off to bed for a nap. Lily Ann opened the refrigerator, then told Josh she had to go shopping.

Not having a grocery list, and being somewhat hungry, she took more time than usual in the supermarket. The back of the Lincoln was full of bulging bags when she pulled into the driveway, but she stopped planning the supper menu the moment she noticed a white station wagon parked in front of the house, an official-looking State of Oklahoma seal on the side. A small, frowning woman stood on the porch jabbing a finger at the doorbell.

Lily Ann drove on past the visitor, expecting that Josh would have answered the door by the time she got inside.

But the sound of impatient chiming, followed by an insistent fist pounding on the door frame, greeted her as she carried in the first load of groceries.

She plunked the sacks onto the table and shot a puzzled look toward the doorway. What on earth was taking Josh so long? As she turned to go investigate, her glance slid over the ceramic countertop.

Instantly she froze, her stomach lurching at the sight of blood smeared on the cream-colored tiles. "Josh!" She squeaked his name in terror. What had happened? Was he okay?

It was easy to see why Josh hadn't wanted Betty Ludlow to come back. Within two minutes of letting the social worker in the front door, Lily Ann had undergone the third degree over exactly who she was and what right she had to be in the Delaney house when there weren't any Delaneys around. When Lily Ann explained the reason she didn't have time to answer a lot of questions, Mrs. Ludlow stormed past her to inspect the bloody kitchen, then announced that one of the children must have been playing with a knife and gotten hurt.

"I *told* him something like this would happen," she said with grim satisfaction. "I asked him how in the world he expected to get them to the hospital when it did. He said his housekeeper could drive." She sniffed. "Where is that woman, anyway—that Rena Leverton?"

"She left six, almost seven weeks ago," Lily Ann answered absently. Doing her own rapid inspection, she noticed the kitchen knife in the sink, a trace of blood on its handle. The side of the sink with the garbage disposal also contained a few shreds of lettuce and small bits of tomatoes and radishes. "Josh was making a salad for supper," she guessed out loud. "He must have cut himself."

Her fear over that was quickly followed by the certainty that he would have called someone to help—most likely Kim Newland, who was home now that school was out for the summer.

"Joshua Delaney...making a salad?" The social worker stared at her over the rims of her bifocals. "Don't be absurd." She shook her head of tightly curled, salt-and-pepper hair. "I should have told someone to keep an eye on this situation while I was out of the office with my surgery. I suspected it would come to this."

Lily Ann was torn between wanting to argue with Mrs. Ludlow and her urgent need to locate Josh. Before she could do either, the telephone shrilled, and she snatched up the receiver at once.

It was Kim, calling from the emergency room. The kids were fine, and Josh would be, too, just as soon as the doctor finished stitching up his thumb. "He says to tell you all the blood he left behind makes it look worse than it really is." She laughed. "Don't ask me how he figured out how bad it looks...although he did bleed for five minutes before I got there. It scared me so bad, I wouldn't take time to leave you a note."

"But he's really okay?"

"He really is. Aside from hounding me to death about calling you so you won't worry, that is. And he's apologetic that he had to put your dinner down the garbage disposal. He didn't think it would be very appetizing after he bled on it."

"Oh, yes, you tell him I'm pretty upset with him that dinner is ruined!" She spoke wryly, blinking back tears and hoping the tremor in her voice would go unnoticed. "Kim, I'm coming to the hospital—"

"No, you're not," Kim said. "I'll probably have these guys back home to you before you finish putting up your groceries. Just please do me a favor and don't be all upset when we get there, okay, kid? Try not to take on over him."

Lily Ann hung up the phone slowly, reminded of Homer, who always called her "kid." And that reminded her of Ned. Her heart heavy, she went about the task of scrubbing off the kitchen cabinet and then bringing in the rest of the purchases from the garage, all but ignoring Mrs. Ludlow, who had taken it upon herself to check out the house.

But when all the bags were emptied, the persistent social worker was waiting for Lily Ann, holding a clipboard of forms that she must have retrieved from her station wagon. "Have a seat," Mrs. Ludlow said with a crisp nod at the table. "I have some questions for you."

Chapter Eleven

By the time Josh and the children arrived home from the hospital, Mrs. Ludlow had gleaned more personal information than Lily Ann had wanted to share. Social Security number. Driver's license number. Bank account data. Date and place of birth. Work history. Family history.

Family history! Lily Ann winced at the way she'd avoided the details of her family life and given Mrs. Ludlow the wrong impressions. But if she'd told the truth, and if Josh ever found out, her world would crumble. And she hadn't dared refuse to answer the social worker's questions. She had a feeling the woman would have punished Josh for Lily Ann's failure to cooperate.

She hated to lie. She absolutely *hated* it! But there'd been no alternative. Mrs. Ludlow had even demanded details about Rena's departure, so Lily Ann had given her an edited version, although one that was basically true—that Rena had up and left on the spur of the moment, going heaven only knew where. Lily Ann simply made no mention of the way the previous housekeeper had tried to cheat Josh.

She'd never been so relieved as she was when her employer walked in holding Kim's elbow with his right hand, his left thumb prominently bandaged. As he greeted Lily Ann, his wary expression told her he knew Mrs. Ludlow was in the room, too. Kim had probably described the station wagon and he'd figured out who the visitor was.

Concerned about his pallor, Lily Ann said, "Sit down, Josh. Let me fix you something to drink." She took a can of V-8 Juice from the pantry, opened it and began filling a glass.

Sarah pulled out a chair at the table. "You sit right here, Uncle Josh," she said in what he called her "little mother" voice. Normally she used it when fussing over her dolls, or over Samuel.

His lips compressed, Josh sat down, and the child stood beside him and patted his knee in an eloquent gesture of reassurance. He put his hand on her shoulder and drew her close, calling in a low voice, "Sam?"

Samuel bounded to his side with all the energy of a four-year-old who'd had a refreshing nap and was ready for action. "Yes, sir?"

"You two go finish unpacking. When your suitcases are empty, put away all your clothes and the things you took to Springfield." He hugged them, an arm around each one, then released them.

They ran out of the room to obey him as Lily Ann put the vegetable juice on the table in front of him. Josh took a drink, then pushed the glass away distractedly.

With an uncertain glance at the silent, watchful social worker, Kim murmured to Josh, "I guess I'll run on home." Passing Lily Ann, with her back to the other woman, she added quietly but emphatically, "Be sure and call if you need me for anything."

The moment Kim had gone, Mrs. Ludlow seemed to reach a decision. She approached Josh with determined steps, placed both palms flat on the table and leaned toward him. "Mr. Delaney, please don't be startled. It's Betty Ludlow from social services."

"Nice to see you again, Mrs. Ludlow," Josh said with dry courtesy.

His composure seemed to bother the social worker, who eyed him uneasily for a moment. "I dropped by for a home visit, to see how things were going, and discovered what happened today," she finally said. "I think it would be best if you let me make arrangements for the care of Sarah and Samuel from now on." She spoke in tones of patronizing helpfulness. "You have plenty to cope with without all the trouble of little ones who don't even belong to you. That's one reason the state has a department of protective services for children."

"You misunderstand the situation in this case, Mrs. Ludlow. Sarah and Samuel may not belong *to* me, but they do belong *with* me, and they're no trouble. Besides, what happened today was no big deal." Josh was still speaking evenly, but Lily Ann suspected that underneath he wasn't so calm. She would have given anything to be able to throw out the meddlesome woman!

"I think it's commendable that you feel responsible for your brother's kids, Mr. Delaney. But you must surely see..." Mrs. Ludlow stopped, a flush coloring her cheeks. "I mean, surely you must grasp that you can't provide the kind of home environment they need. What if they had been injured today because of your, er, visual limitations?"

"Why should they have been injured? I was the one using the knife."

"Yes, I'm aware of that." Disapproval crept into her voice. "There's another reason our department exists—to step in and take over when adults exercise poor judgment, resulting in the abuse or neglect of children."

Josh pushed back his chair and started to stand up, then thought better of it. A muscle twitched along his jaw. "Sarah and Samuel have never in their lives been neglected or abused."

"Oh, I'm not saying you did it on purpose," the state worker hastened to add. As if she knew Lily Ann was about to jump into the fray, she shot her a distrustful look before regarding Josh again with fretful concern. "I believe you're doing the best you can. But you can't do it alone, and your hired help isn't what I would call reliable." She cleared her throat. "Frankly, Mr. Delaney, your track record when it comes to housekeepers isn't very good. Mildred Brown was an excellent caregiver, but she had the misfortune of dying. Then you hired Rena Leverton." She sniffed disdainfully. "Besides not knowing one end of a mop from the other, she walked out without giving notice. And your current housekeeper . . . well, suffice to say the bedrooms were a mess when I peeked at them earlier."

Before Lily Ann could say a word, Josh defended her. "Come back tomorrow and look again. We've been out of town and haven't got everything unpacked."

"You've taken a trip together?" The question was even frostier than the woman's earlier observations. "I don't think you could have selected a more inappropriate housekeeper if you had tried. Miss Jones is young, inexperienced and worst of all, extremely attractive. It's a

wonder the entire town isn't talking about what's going on
here. Taking trips together, indeed!''

Lily Ann's mouth fell open and her heart thundered. She
couldn't believe what she was hearing. Did people think
they'd been sleeping together? Oh, Lord, was it possible
someone had found out she loved Josh?

"There's nothing going on here for anyone to gossip
about!'' Josh spoke through clenched teeth. This time he
did stand up, his right hand gripping the edge of the table
so nobody would guess how light-headed he was feeling.
"Don't you even care that Sarah and Samuel love her?
Doesn't it count for anything that since she came we've had
three good meals a day and that Lily Ann usually keeps the
house so clean you could eat off the floors? Just what kind
of woman would you consider appropriate for the job?''

"Someone who isn't going to fall in love with the first
handsome young man who takes her dancing or out to the
movies,'' Mrs. Ludlow said bluntly. "Someone mature
enough not to get bored with nothing to entertain her but
a blind man and two children.''

"I'm not going to get bored!''

Ignoring Lily Ann's hot protest, the other woman spoke
directly to Josh. "This is an unhealthy environment for
your niece and nephew, Mr. Delaney. With a stream of
undependable housekeepers flitting in and out of their
lives, they will never feel secure. And you can never know
for sure that Miss Jones will be here when you wake up in
the morning, can you?''

Lily Ann turned to Josh and, seeing the look on his face,
grabbed his arm and shook it a little. "Josh, I am *not* going to leave!''

"Even if she stays,'' Mrs. Ludlow went on ruthlessly,
"what the children need for a stable childhood are two
parents. Not a housekeeper and an uncle who's unable to

care for them by himself. It doesn't matter how good your intentions are, Mr. Delaney. They need parents who can see. Parents who can keep them safe, look out for them, show them how to do things."

Her breath catching at the pain she could read in Josh's expression, Lily Ann tightened her hold on his wrist. "Don't listen to her, Josh!"

Josh stood perfectly still, waiting for the next verbal blow to fall. When it came, it was a bit softer, rife with sympathy, but no less devastating.

"I'm afraid, Mr. Delaney, that I'm going to have to take action on behalf of the children. It seems to me that a full-scale investigation is called for here. I'm going to speak with the judge about taking legal measures to remove Sarah and Samuel from your guardianship. We can place them in foster homes where they'll be well cared for, I assure you, so you're not to worry..."

Her head throbbing dully and her stomach tied up in knots, Lily Ann stacked the last of the supper dishes in the dishwasher and turned it on, then gave the room a cursory glance to be sure it was in order before she left the kitchen. On her way down the hall, she paused at the door of the study. Tears welled in her eyes as she stood there gazing at Josh, who sat with his injured hand resting palm up on the desk in front of him, a brooding look on his face. He seemed so...so unreachable, so lost in thought, but she knew he had to be absolutely shattered by Mrs. Ludlow's heartless decision to remove Sarah and Samuel from the only home they'd ever known.

After the social worker had gone, and all the time supper was cooking, Lily Ann had tried to draw some reaction out of him. She'd talked herself hoarse, expressing her angry disgust with self-righteous bureaucrats who ruined lives by thinking they knew what was best for everybody else.

"Where does she get off, implying you aren't a good father?" Lily Ann had demanded of Josh. "She doesn't know beans about our situation!" She wasn't sure when it had become "our" situation and had ceased to be just Josh and the children's. Maybe when Betty Ludlow predicted that Lily Ann would grow bored and split. "I'm not going to leave, Josh," she insisted. "I'm here for the long haul. That woman doesn't have a clue about me."

Stone-faced and tense, Josh had made no reply.

Even a phone call from his editor hadn't touched him. He hadn't seemed to hear Lily Ann when she told him Phillip McKay wanted to talk to him about the partial manuscript they had mailed to New York before leaving town last week. She had finally been forced to make excuses to Mr. McKay, who had stayed late at the office to finish reading the chapters and was eager to see the completed book. "Ask Josh to call me back first thing tomorrow," the man had instructed her, and she'd promised to convey the message, while warning him that Josh had rather pressing issues on his mind.

Watching him now, Lily Ann wanted to break down and cry, she was so frightened. Instead, she blinked back her tears and spoke up as matter-of-factly as she could. "Josh, won't you please let me call a lawyer for you? We have to fight this. We can't just sit here and take it!"

Josh shifted his head toward her. "Lily Ann? I thought you'd gone to bed." Rousing himself, he opened his watch and checked the time. "You need to get some rest. We can talk tomorrow."

Tomorrow! Tomorrow might be too late! Didn't he realize...

With supreme effort she got a grip on her impotent, terrified fury. Of course he realized. Josh had everything at stake here. If he lost the children, he would be losing what he cared about most in life.

"You need your rest, too, after all that's happened today." Her voice was subdued. "Is your hand hurting?"

"It's fine. I'll go to bed soon." As an afterthought he added, "You can turn off the light. If you leave it on, I'll probably forget."

Lily Ann hesitated, then did as he asked, her eyes burning as she went on to her bedroom. She always felt wretched when she discovered Josh sitting in the dark by himself. It was a grim reminder of his blindness that she didn't need. But what she should remember was that he didn't need the light. It made no difference to him if the lamp was on or off.

Trying not to think about what Mrs. Ludlow planned to do, she took a couple of aspirin and crawled between the sheets. After a while the pounding in her temples abated and she slept.

A light flooding the room snatched her abruptly out of her anxious dreams. She sat up in bed and stared at Josh where he stood framed in her doorway. "What's the matter?" she asked quickly. "Is it your thumb?"

Josh had forgotten all about his thumb, despite the throbbing inside the deep cut. He shook his head and began cautiously making his way toward the bed, toward the sound of her voice. Not having been in here lately, he wasn't sure how Lily Ann had the furniture arranged. "We have to talk."

Now he wanted to talk! Lily Ann watched him approach, his right hand outstretched. Her pulse had revved up the moment she awoke, and now her heart turned a nervous flip. Josh was wearing just a pair of baggy, white cotton pajama trousers that Lily Ann had laundered any number of times but had never before seen on his long legs. She couldn't possibly have anticipated how she would feel, seeing the drawstring knotted at his lean waist to keep the pants up, his bare shoulders and arms and chest brown and firmly muscled.

Closing her eyes, she swallowed hard against the gnawing sharpness of her hunger, then looked again just as his shin bumped the end of her bed. "Here, Josh," she said, getting onto her knees to take his hand and direct him around the side.

He sank onto the edge of the bed and faced the door, his profile to her. His dark hair was almost standing on end. When he released her hand, he raised his own and dragged it through the gleaming, satiny curls, leaving them more tousled than ever. "I'm sorry I woke you up."

"It's okay, Josh." She locked her hands together on her lap to keep from reestablishing the contact with him. "What did you need?"

"I have to tell you something." Bracing his arms straight, he dug his fingers into the mattress on either side of him. "It's about a little girl named Laura." His voice was strangely urgent. "Laura's father disappeared before she was born, and when she was still pretty small her mother started drinking too much. I guess it was her way of coping with a hard, unhappy life. Besides being unable to hold a job and getting by on public assistance, the mother was in and out of hospitals for her alcoholism for years, always leaving the child with neighbors when she committed herself."

Lily Ann listened raptly, able to imagine all too well what that must have been like for the youngster. "When Laura was ten," Josh was saying, "her mother vanished just the way her father had done. The neighbors called in

child welfare, and the state took over that little girl's life."
He hunched his shoulders. "Before she went out on her
own at seventeen, she lived in twelve foster homes and two
places that I guess you'd call orphanages. Despite the
kindness of some of the foster parents—despite the fact
that nobody was to blame—it was hell on earth for Laura.
She never belonged anywhere...she always felt like a
burden. The system just didn't work in her case. She always kept praying her mother would come back for her,
even though the woman had never shown her much affection. Not until Laura met Jeff, years later, did she ever
have a sense of being loved and wanted for herself."

Laura...and Jeff? He was talking about his brother's
wife?

Josh half twisted toward Lily Ann, reaching out to find
her hand. His long, restless fingers closed around her arm,
then slid down her wrist and laced with her fingers. "I
can't let that happen to Sarah and Samuel, Lily Ann. I
won't let it happen!" Intensity roughened his tone. "You
probably think Jeff and Laura were crazy not to change
their wills after my accident. I thought so myself until I
talked to them about it. I couldn't imagine them still
wanting me to be the children's guardian if anything happened to them. But Laura insisted they'd be better off here
with me than bouncing from pillar to post, never belong-
ing. Even if I couldn't see."

Her eyes misting, Lily Ann cleared her throat and did
her best to steady her voice. "That's what I've been saying, Josh. I told you not to listen to that old busybody."

"Yeah, well, that old busybody was right about one
thing." His chin sank to his chest and muffled his next
words. "Kids stand a better chance for a good life if they
have two parents. Sarah and Sam don't just need an uncle
and a housekeeper."

"But Josh—"

He tightened his grip on her hand and lifted his head. "Let me finish while I still have the nerve. They need two parents, even if one parent happens to be blind." There was an electric pause. "They're good kids, Lily Ann, and they love you, perhaps more than you suspect. You've become an important part of their lives. I'm not saying this to make you feel under any kind of obligation, but just so you'll realize how well you fit in here. If we were to get married ... if you were to marry me, I really believe we could persuade Judge Robbins that this would be the best place for the kids."

Her heart tumbling over, Lily Ann seemed to stop breathing. He had just proposed that they get married! Stunned hope and joy flooded through her as she stared at his beloved face, bent toward her as if watching for her response.

It was the answer to her prayers. To be Josh's wife—to be a real and permanent part of this family—would be the fulfillment of a beautiful dream. It had been dawning on her for a while that since she'd come to work for Josh, she'd been happier than any other time of her life, and she never wanted to leave ... never wanted to have to say goodbye to Josh and Sarah and Samuel. She loved them, each one. Especially Josh. A radiant smile lit her face as she gazed at him, feeling love tug at her heart.

And then slowly the smile faded and despair gripped Lily Ann. Josh hadn't proposed because he loved her. *Loved* her! Dear Lord, he could only *hate* her if he knew who she was! If she married him, the truth would surely come out sooner or later, and then he would grow to despise her. He would despise her just as he almost certainly despised her father for causing his blindness. And she didn't think she could bear the pain of Josh's hatred.

Josh heard Lily Ann's soft gasp, then felt her fingers stiffen within his, all the warmth seeping out of them. As her hand chilled, it was like having a bucket of ice water poured over his head. What in the world had he been thinking, to suggest that she marry him? He was pretty close to desperate to save the kids, yes, but had he lost his mind? He must have been delusional to think she would ever marry him. He was blind!

Suddenly feeling as if every square inch of his skin was on fire, he pulled his hand free and got to his feet. "That was a stupid idea," he muttered as he made for the door.

"Josh, wait!" Lily Ann scrambled after him and caught his sun-bronzed forearm to stop him, then stood in anguished uncertainty, hearing the drumbeat of her own heart as she searched his face. She knew what he was thinking—it was etched clearly on his features. And he was so wrong!

"Just forget what I said, Lily Ann," he said tautly. "It's not your problem."

"Oh, Josh, you can't believe that! I love those kids, too. I want it to be my problem."

She really was upset, he thought, otherwise she never would have expressed her feelings so honestly.

His voice softened. "I'll think of something. You go back to bed."

"No!" Fear sharpened the word. She didn't know what she would do if Josh ever found out her deepest, darkest secret, but she did know she couldn't let him go on thinking she was rejecting him because he couldn't see. The rest of their lives were at stake—Josh's, the children's, her own. For the chance to marry Josh and spend her life with him, or even part of her life, she was willing to risk anything.

Mustering all the humor she could, she said, "For Pete's sake, can't you show a little patience? That's the first proposal I've had in a year. I needed to think about it a minute." An unconscious note of gravity slipped into her voice. "Now that I've thought it over, I believe your idea just might work. This would certainly be a more stable environment for Sarah and Samuel than being shuttled around from one foster home to another."

He was listening, some strong emotion contracting his throat muscles, his thick lashes flickering briefly to veil his smoky eyes.

Please, God, she prayed, *help me convince him!*

"After all, we've been functioning as a family in nearly every other way," she threw in as casually as possible. "Why not make it official?"

Chapter Twelve

Josh had just checked his watch for the fifth time in as many minutes when he heard the door to the minister's study open. His head snapped up, and his right hand clamped reflexively onto the arm of the chair where he was sitting. "Grover?"

"Yep. Me again. Try to settle down, Josh. What are you so jumpy for, anyway?"

Josh's frown asked what, indeed! "We were supposed to get started at seven and it's already a quarter past. How much longer will it be?"

Grover took a seat on the sofa nearby and began absently rummaging through his pockets until he remembered where he'd put the ring. "Well, it may be a little while. Reverend Oliver thinks we should wait until people stop arriving. You know...just to be polite."

He lifted an eyebrow. "People are still coming?"

"By the dozens." The banker sounded cheerful.

"I thought you said just a few would show up!"

"No, what I said was, it might be short notice, but your friends and neighbors would want to be included, and obviously I was right. It looks like half the town is crowding into the church."

Propping his chin on his fist, Josh exhaled bleakly. "Letting you get involved was a mistake. I should have stuck with my original plan and kept this simple and quick."

"You asked me to take you shopping for the ring and help you get the license, remember? That's not exactly going overboard. Besides, what do you mean, quick? You only gave me three days—"

"Yeah, well, you've managed to do plenty of damage in three days. Dragging in half the town," he muttered under his breath.

"I didn't drag in a single soul. Everybody's so happy for you, they all invited themselves." Grover gave Josh a playful punch on the shoulder. "And this is the thanks I get! You call it damage! Anyway, you'll change your tune when you see the wedding gifts piling up in the foyer."

"I'm not getting married in order to get gifts. And I have to tell you, I don't look forward to entertaining a packed house. It's bad enough bumping into things when nobody's watching." Josh fidgeted, then stood up and stretched. "I just want to get this over with and get back home."

His friend chuckled dryly. "I imagine you do! So would I, if I were about to marry Lily Ann."

The reminder silenced Josh. He sank back into the chair and made himself think one more time about what he was doing tonight. He was committing himself in a way he'd never seriously considered until just recently. He was binding his life to that of a woman who smelled like the very essence of heaven, who reminded him of a walking dream, whose voice and touch sent warm shivers of plea-sure dancing up and down his spine. But it was the *why* that he needed to keep in focus. He was doing this for Sarah and Samuel. For Laura and Jeff. Because he'd promised to take care of the kids.

Liar! he accused himself. He was doing it most of all for Joshua Delaney. The thought of losing Sarah and Samuel made him literally sick; he wasn't sure what would give purpose to his existence if they didn't need him anymore. And the idea that at some point in the future Lily Ann would quit her job and go away cut him to the quick with despair. He wanted to know she would be within his reach forever.

Clearing his throat, he strove to sound normal. "Where are Sarah and Sam?"

"They're with Lily Ann, waiting to come down the aisle with her. She's got them all dressed up in their Sunday best, looking like a couple of angels. And man alive, Josh, I wish you could see how Lily Ann looks in her long white gown...."

Josh managed a short nod. Ever since he met her, he'd been wishing he could see how she looked. But almost more than that, he wished she had someone to escort her to the altar... a father, or a brother, or even a distant cousin. It wasn't good for her to be so completely on her own at a time like this. When Josh had asked if there wasn't at least some old family friend who could give her away, she hesitated long enough for him to know she was considering someone; then she said rather vaguely that she'd lost touch with all her old family friends. Josh didn't think he believed her.

Grover Thomason was to be best man and Kim New-land the matron of honor. Kim had volunteered Paul to walk Lily Ann down the aisle—a move that made Josh feel inclined to hug the generous kindergarten teacher, and her husband, too, when he seconded the idea. But then Lily Ann suggested that Paul usher in the guests instead, insisting that having Sarah and Samuel beside her would give her all the support she needed. Josh could only hope her courage wouldn't fail her....

When the organist finally played the opening chords of the Bridal March, Lily Ann said a silent prayer of thanks for her small attendants. The church was packed, mostly with people she didn't know, but the little girl and boy on either side of her kept throwing her smiles so full of happy pride that her nervousness vanished, replaced by warm contentment. She lifted her eyes and saw the handsome, black-haired man in the tuxedo waiting—not watching for her, but tilting his head in an attitude of listening intently—and hopeful expectation bubbled up inside her. She could hardly keep her steps slow enough to match the dignified tempo of the processional.

Her eyes firmly fixed on Josh, Lily Ann made it down to the front. While Kim led Sarah and Samuel to one side, she took her place next to Josh and touched his arm. Finding her hand, he locked his fingers with hers. Despite the awkward bandage on his thumb, the pressure of his grip both reassured her and questioned how she was holding up. Giving his injured hand a careful squeeze, she blinked away the sudden tears that threatened her composure.

She really thought she might lose it a moment later when Reverend Oliver began his introduction to the marriage ritual. "We read in the Psalms that God sets the lonely in families," the minister said, "and so He is doing with Josh and Lily Ann tonight."

Yes! she thought and nearly started crying out of pure joy. That was it! That was exactly what had happened to her! She'd been lonely much of her life; her hunger for a home and the kind of family that could be counted on was a secret part of her she'd never shared with anyone. It was perhaps the very deepest need of her soul. And now, in some kind of miracle, she was receiving both home and family!

As Josh repeated the sacred vows, she concentrated so hard on them, it was almost as if they were being engraved on her heart. When her turn came, she promised with everything that was in her to love, honor and cherish him. Knowing nothing could ever bring her to break such a commitment, she prayed that Josh would take it just as seriously. They might have unusual reasons for getting married, but as far as she was concerned, this was for life.

The next thing she knew the minister had pronounced them man and wife. With measured movements, Josh was lifting her veil and framing her face with his hands, his right thumb caressing her lips lightly until his mouth swooped down to claim the traditional kiss.

Like those he'd given her previously, this kiss went straight to her heart and set it pounding harder than ever. Her heated blood rushed helter-skelter through her veins, her breathing became erratic and her knees grew perilously weak. It felt something like getting zapped by lightning, she thought dazedly, clutching his arms with both hands to keep from staggering in front of everyone.

When he raised his head, she was still sizzling inside, melting in the most intriguing and enjoyable way possible. All she could do was whisper in wonder, "Josh!"

He wore an odd expression, as if he was highly pleased by the kiss and at the same time jolted by it. She supposed it had been more electrifying than either of them had been expecting.

His dark lashes drifted downward as he gave her a slow, heart-stopping smile. "Later," he whispered, responding to something he must have heard in her voice when she breathed his name.

The promise brought a flush to her cheeks. They both wanted the same thing, even though she hadn't even realized that was the message her husky tone had conveyed.

"Can you get us out of here?" he asked in words for her ears only.

She could and did. Outside the church, although mobbed by friends offering hearty congratulations, Josh never let go of her arm. Both would have preferred to be transported away magically with the snap of a finger, but some ladies, organized by Kim and the minister's wife, had put together a reception with delicate finger sandwiches, cake and punch.

After all the trouble the neighbors had gone to, Josh and Lily Ann felt obliged to put in an appearance. They dutifully ate a few bites, but when Lily Ann slipped away shortly to change clothes, nobody seemed surprised. She'd bought her wedding gown off the rack at a bridal shop in Bartlesville, along with the simply cut yellow silk sheath that she donned now. Just as she finished brushing her thick blond hair and fastening it back from both temples with tortoiseshell combs, Kim brought Sarah and Samuel into the dressing room to tell Lily Ann goodbye. The children were excited about staying with Kim and Paul until the newlyweds returned from the brief honeymoon they'd planned.

"We'll miss you and Uncle Josh, though," Sarah assured Lily Ann as they embraced.

"We're going to miss you, too, honey. But we'll only be gone a couple of days."

"This many?" Samuel held up a hand with fingers splayed.

"No, love, *this* many." She tucked down all but his chubby index and middle fingers. "Count 'em for me, Samuel."

"One, two. Two nights?"

"Right. We'll be home on Sunday." She hugged him and kissed his soft cheek, and he squeezed her back with all his might.

"Is it okay if we call you Aunt Lily Ann now?" Sarah asked, watching Lily Ann stroke her brother's hair.

Pleasure swept through her and she grinned at her new niece and nephew. "It's better than okay. I'd like that very much!"

Still heady with satisfaction a few minutes later, she and Josh left the church amid a hail of birdseed and shouted best wishes and began the forty-five mile trip to Tulsa. She was driving the Lincoln, with Josh seated beside her looking both weary and relieved. Just about the time they left the Bartlesville city limits, he settled back more comfortably against the seat, dropped his head onto the padded headrest, stretched out his long legs and sighed.

Since his eyes were almost closed and his mouth curved in a relaxed half smile, she expected him to fall asleep, so when he spoke after twenty miles of silence it made her jump. "I wish you—" Stopping abruptly, he began again. "Sorry. I didn't mean to startle you."

His perception of her reactions and moods just kept getting sharper all the time.

"It's okay, Josh." She sent him a reluctant glance of admiration across the darkened interior of the car. Joshua Delaney held such a strong appeal for her, it was hard to keep her eyes off him, even in a light no better than the dashboard's eerie glow. It was harder still to forget his murmured "Later!" after the potent kiss they'd shared at the altar; she'd been trying for the past half hour, but his familiar scent in the enclosed car and his incredible personal magnetism made it impossible.

Not wanting him to know where her mind had been, she offered an excuse that was partly true. "I needed to be snapped out of my trance. You know how the highway stripes can sort of hypnotize you when you stare at them mile after mile?"

He nodded thoughtfully. "You must be as tired as I am. I was just going to say, I wish you didn't have to do all the driving whenever we go anywhere."

Despite the lump that formed in her throat she managed to respond nonchalantly. "Don't give it another thought, Josh! I like to drive. Remember where we were this time last week?"

Turning his head in her direction, he seemed to be trying to discipline his twitching lips. "Our destination isn't the only thing different about this trip, Lily Ann."

Her careless pose failed her. "I know!" Boy, did she ever know!

He remained silent for a while before he asked, without a trace of amusement now, "Any regrets?"

He must be able to tell how scared she was. He just hadn't guessed the secret that made her so scared. She took a deep breath. "No regrets. What about you?"

After a slight hesitation, he shrugged one broad shoulder. "Just that you didn't have any family or friends here with you."

For the second time his quiet concern for her knocked her off balance. She swallowed hard. "No big deal," she said, the catch in her voice giving it a gruff quality. "Anyway, your best friend couldn't make it, either. I know you wanted him to be here."

Josh shrugged again. "At least by this time Kael knows
Mildred died, since we wrote him in Calcutta." His
thoughts produced a devilish, utterly irresistible grin.
"Let's send him a postcard and tell him we're on our honeymoon. That should get him back here on the double."

His low, easy chuckle did something to the nerve endings in her stomach. She'd never heard a laugh that she
liked as well . . . a laugh that made her feel hot and cold all
over . . . a laugh that stirred up this primitive want inside her
and made her think about laying her hand over his throat,
and then his chest, and then his abdomen, to find out exactly which was the source of such a sexy sound.

By the time they reached Tulsa and located the hotel
where they had reservations, Lily Ann had started shaking. Josh had to feel it when he took her arm to walk inside.

At the desk in the elegant lobby, he paid for the room
and she signed the guest registry in a wobbly script, having to scratch out and start over when she muffed her new
signature. Josh heard her expel her breath in chagrin, then
apologize to the desk clerk.

"That's all right," the man said in an indulgent tone
that he probably saved for flustered newlyweds. "By the
way, may I extend the congratulations of the management
to you both, Mr. and Mrs. Delaney? You'll find a basket
of fruit in your room, compliments of the house, when the
bellboy takes you up."

With an absentminded thanks, Josh accompanied Lily
Ann half a dozen steps in what he figured was the direction of the elevators before he halted. That stopped her,
too, and she turned her head to look back up at him. "Did
we forget something?"

Hearing the footsteps of the porter going on ahead, Josh
released her arm and cut straight to the heart of the mat-

ter. "You're uncomfortable with this, Lily Ann. Should we get two rooms?"

She pivoted to face him. "Two rooms?" she repeated blankly. Then, "Oh! Oh, no...not unless you...you don't want..."

Her words trailed off. She could see from his expression that there was no problem with *his* wanting. She could also see that he would never demand more than she wanted to give.

"Josh, I...I expected to share your room and...your bed."

One corner of his mouth quirked in a wry grimace. Other than that he didn't move.

Her cheeks aflame, she reached for his hand, which felt stiff, and tucked it through her arm. "It's not a problem for me. Honestly."

Still he held back, his muscles unresponsive.

The rangy, youthful bellboy had gone all the way to the elevators with the luggage before noticing that he was alone. Lily Ann figured that in about ten seconds he would start backtracking to collect his wayward hotel guests.

She muttered quickly, hoarsely, "Lord, Josh, you're going to make me spell it out, aren't you? Okay! I don't *want* separate rooms." What the heck, she thought. She'd gone this far, she might as well go the whole distance. "I'm your wife, and I want a chance to act like it. By the same token, I expect you to act like my husband. Am I making myself clear?"

Josh had heard what she hadn't—the porter's footsteps returning. A trace of tender amusement softened his mouth just before the hotel employee convulsed into an embarrassed fit of coughing behind her.

"Perfectly clear," Josh murmured, taking a firmer grip on her arm to follow her once more.

Although the honeymoon suite hadn't been available on such short notice, the room they ended up with was lovely. Besides the fruit basket, a vase of fresh flowers stood on the dresser, perfuming the air with its ambrosial blend of fragrances. When the disconcerted baggage handler had departed, Lily Ann helped Josh acquaint himself with the spacious accommodations.

After that, while she watched with silent fascination, Josh took off his suit jacket and hung it in the closet, then unknotted his tie and pulled it off. With one hand slowly undoing his shirt buttons, he moved until he faced her near the end of the bed, both of them aware that there was nothing left to delay the natural progression of events.

His unfocused eyes a darker gray than usual, Josh reached out and touched his fingertips to her shoulder, stroked the rich material of her dress assessingly, then slid his palm down her bare arm. Her pulse leaped at the sensation, even as she saw twin sparks leap in his eyes. His lashes flickering, he raised his hand and curved it against her smooth cheek.

"You look even more beautiful than usual tonight, Lily Ann," he said, his voice husky.

The feel of his thumb teasing the corner of her lips sent a shiver of unbelievable excitement rippling through her. "In Sarah's opinion?" she asked as lightly as she could.

"Mmm...And Grover's, Kim's, Paul's, Reverend Oliver's...just about everybody at the wedding. They all made sure I know how lucky I am." His voice dropped. "As it happens, I already knew that." Lifting his other hand, he threaded the fingers into the silken thickness of her hair, then held her in place while he brought his mouth down onto hers.

The kiss compelled her closer to him. Just that gentle contact drew her into a slow spin and pulled her down,

down, down into a sea of molten sensation so pure and achingly tender it took her breath away. Engulfed by a feeling of overwhelming love for Josh, she slid her hands beneath his unbuttoned shirt and clasped them together behind his smoothly muscled back. Then she molded herself to his warm steely length while he nibbled at the sweetness of her lips.

His mouth grazed over her skin, kindling a white-hot flame inside her. The flame glowed even hotter and brighter as Josh ran his hands down her neck and shoulders, then behind her to begin undoing the buttons on her dress. The trembling of his fingers and the unsteady pounding of his heart pressed right against hers made her want him more than ever, when she already wanted him so much it hurt.

After he'd succeeded in slipping her dress off, his lips trailed down her throat, into the valley between her breasts, then back up to the soft, vulnerable spot just behind her ear. His strong arms enfolded her and he held her tightly, his breath a deep sigh of agony. "Oh, Lily Ann," he managed to groan, "it feels like I've been waiting for this forever!"

Me, too! she wanted to cry but couldn't. Shy uncertainty and long habit stopped her. Instead, she blinked away the tears as fast as they gathered on her lashes. "No more waiting, Josh," she whispered hoarsely and pulled back to unbuckle his belt.

Chapter Thirteen

Lily Ann awoke Saturday morning lying snuggled up as close as she could get to Josh, with his arms wrapped around her and his face buried in her hair. She felt his breath warming her neck and his fingers slowly, gently combing through the curtain of silken strands that fanned across her bare shoulders.

As she lay enjoying the fluid sensations that he evoked and gazing around at the sunshine filtering into the hotel room, it all came back to her: the delicious fulfillment of the night before when she and Josh had made tender love for hours...the security and satisfaction of being able to reach for him when she awoke deep in the night...the rekindling of embers into flaming passion when he woke up, too, and began to trace her features with his curious, beguiling fingertips...

Smiling with secret joy, she yawned and stretched just for the thrill of brushing against his bare, hair-roughened, distinctly masculine shape. That one leisurely moment of warm friction was enough to send a shudder of sensual bliss rocketing through her.

When Josh felt her move, his hand paused in mid-stroke. "Good morning, Lily Ann Delaney."

Her smile grew as she considered the sound of her new name. "Good morning right back to you, Joshua Cole Delaney."

His mouth nuzzled her ear, and he mumbled something.

She shivered again. *No,* she thought, *he couldn't have said what I thought he said!* She must have misunderstood.

"Excuse me?" she asked, then waited breathlessly.

"I love you," he repeated in a low, husky voice.

"Me?" she gasped.

"You."

All of a sudden her heart was pounding so hard, she feared it would shatter the nearest ribs. He loved her!

Tears pricked her eyes, and she tried to staunch them by making light of things. "Why, Josh...this is so sudden! How long have you known?"

"Almost as long as I've known you. Your voice got to me first. Then your scent. And then I touched you." He sounded half serious, half ironic, and when she tipped back her head to see his face, she found that he wore an expression of self-mocking humor. "I couldn't get enough, especially of the touching. My fingers had never brailled anyone as beautiful as you."

"You love me because I'm beautiful?"

"Mmm-hmm. Because you're as beautiful on the inside as you are on the outside."

Her tears welled in earnest. What a remarkable thing to say to her! But how could she respond? She loved Josh, too—loved him so much, in fact, that hearing him declare his love for her was beyond her wildest dreams.

But she was filled with a terrible shame at the way she had deceived him. He'd married her thinking she was somebody else—having no idea who she really was. And she couldn't tell him.

"Josh, I...I..." *I love you...want you...need you! Please don't ever, ever stop loving me!*

"Hmm?"

Oh, Lord! What was wrong with her? She couldn't even tell him how she felt! "I, uh, guess we'd better get moving if we're going to make it to both the Philbrook and the Gilcrease Museums...."

Was he disappointed in what she didn't say? She watched him as she got out of bed and he followed a bit more slowly, cautious in an unfamiliar bedroom. His face reflected patience...or did that look mean he was merely resigned? Anguish contracted her throat as she wondered.

He explored the neatly packed suitcase until he found his shaving kit and lifted it out. "If you want to shower first, I can be shaving."

I love you! her heart cried without a sound.

"Josh?" She spoke hesitantly. "How about if we shower together?"

She was rewarded by his swift agreement and the delighted grin that washed away every other emotion.

That day and the next were ones she knew she would never forget. After an immensely gratifying shower, they got dressed, then went out and explored museums and parks and historic churches, shopped in antique galleries and a mall with an ice-skating rink, ate at little out-of-the-way restaurants and—when Josh announced that he was famished—at the nearest available food place, a bustling, noisy McDonald's. Saturday evening they went to an outdoor performance of the Rodgers and Hammerstein musical *Oklahoma!*, then went back to the hotel and made love far into the night. On Sunday they played tourist again.

Although each moment they shared seemed precious to Lily Ann, she was strangely preoccupied and her throat ached the whole time... ached with words she couldn't quite say. *I love you, Josh!* She'd guarded her heart too long, afraid of being hurt, of caring too much.

Why couldn't she just spill it out? Josh was telling her he loved her, not just with words but with gestures, when he bought her flowers from a vender at the mall, and when he risked eating a Big Mac and fries in a setting that would have horrified him before he started going places with Lily Ann, and when he lifted her hand to kiss it during an especially tender scene in the musical. The thought that he couldn't possibly know she loved him, too, brought tears to her eyes every time she thought about it.

The tears became a real problem as she was driving them back to Bartlesville late Sunday afternoon. She kept having to dab at her eyes with a tissue, and once she had to pull the car over onto the shoulder of the highway. "The sun's in my eyes," she lied when he asked what the problem was.

Josh compressed his lips, then quickly schooled his features to hide his frown. The last thing he meant to do was pressure her to open up to him. Obviously she didn't want to tell him what was bothering her. One thing he knew: it wasn't the sun—unless someone had changed the direction of the highway from what it used to be back when he could drive, he thought wryly. There was no way the setting sun could be in her eyes on a road that led due north.

Stretching out in a convincing picture of relaxed unconcern, he laced his fingers together behind his head and closed his eyes. Once the car was moving again, he brought up what he figured was a safe topic. "We'll have to take the kids and go back to Tulsa in a few weeks."

They'd talked about this already. The fact that Sarah and Samuel would enjoy the Tulsa Zoo was the one thing that had kept Josh and Lily Ann from visiting it on this trip. They wanted to save it for a time when the children were with them.

Lily Ann responded absentmindedly...not with the enthusiastic agreement Josh had hoped for.

"Of course, we still haven't taken them to the petting zoo at Woolaroc," he added.

"Mmm..." she mumbled.

With a smothered sigh, Josh let the conversation drop. Neither spoke again until she had turned the Lincoln into a familiar driveway, then raised the electric door and pulled into the garage. "Home," he said quietly.

She made a small sound that might have been a muffled sob. Frustration clamped down on his muscles, but he got out of the car in silence and carried in the heaviest piece of luggage. While Lily Ann unloaded the rest, Josh stepped out onto the back porch and stood there with his head back, dragging in deep breaths as he lectured himself on the importance of being patient. She always kept her emotions under strict control; it was one of the first things he'd learned about her. He could hardly expect her to change overnight, if at all.

Gradually a calm settled over him. The fragrant air helped, redolent of appealing country smells like freshly tilled earth and grass that had just been cut. Herman had said he would do the yard while they were gone. The roses climbing the back fence must have been in full bloom, because their fragrance had drifted clear to the house....

All of a sudden Lily Ann was beside him, slipping her hand into his and gripping his fingers as if clutching a lifeline. "Josh, I . . . I . . ." She paused, her breathing ragged. "I love you!"

The instant the words were out, relief flooded her. She'd done it, and it felt *wonderful*—as if a ten-ton weight had been lifted off her back.

Anxiously she studied him to see how he had taken the news. He tilted his head to one side as if looking at her, his eyes hooded, his mouth grave, and she wasn't sure he believed her.

"I do, Josh," she insisted softly. "I love you!"

"Shh . . ." He turned and touched his fingertips to her lips, stopping her words. Then he gathered her to him with both arms and held her for a long time against his chest, still not speaking. The strong, steady rhythm of his heart reassured her and gave her hope.

That night, after they put Sarah and Samuel to bed, she told him again, and again early in the morning while they were making love in Josh's big bed—her bed, too, now. The words grew easier each time, and she just kept feeling lighter and more elated.

With the clarity that came from being in love, she soon began to see Josh with new eyes. Where once she might have felt wretched and guilty that blindness made him spend much of his time at home, she watched him with the children and discovered that he had a closeness to them that few other parents, or parent substitutes, achieved. Sarah and Samuel, having always had him near at hand, worked him into most of their games. He helped them build every imaginable sort of structure out of Lego and Tinkertoys and plain old sand. He told them stories to cheer them up, or to illustrate a lesson, or just to put them to sleep. He held them, rocked them, kissed away their hurts and made sure they knew he loved and valued them. The bond between man and children would last forever.

Where she might have felt sad at all the strict limits imposed on his life, instead she came to appreciate how well he knew his own world, and how much progress he was making in accepting the limitations. He no longer seemed so frustrated when he stumbled. Indeed, one day he used his cane and walked to Kim's house when she called to say she'd just baked some chocolate chip cookies for the Delaneys.

"Why didn't you tell me?" Lily Ann demanded when he finally made it back home, hot and sweaty from the midday June sun. "It wouldn't have taken me five minutes to run over and get the cookies."

"You were cleaning house and watching the kids," he said with an offhand shrug. "I needed the exercise."

"But it took you an hour and a half!"

He just grinned and wiped his sleeve across his damp face. "So what? There's a Chinese proverb that says, 'Be not afraid of going slowly, be afraid only of standing still.'"

Stand still? *Josh?* she mused with good-humored admiration. Not likely—not in anything! Just as in writing...he might have had to adapt to another way of putting the words down, but write he would. And judging from his editor's reaction to the chapters of the uncompleted book, Josh would be a success at this new phase in his career. Phillip McKay was already talking contracts and advances.

Josh had accomplished a lot in spite of some pretty formidable obstacles. Maybe...maybe her father hadn't ruined his life after all.

After examining the idea suspiciously and at length, she had to admit that nobody with any degree of perception could describe Josh's life as ruined. He had too much going for him...too many who adored and looked up to him. He'd developed strength of character when the alternatives were bitterness and self-pity. Because he'd faced his challenges, he was a better person than he otherwise might have been.

Maybe she could quit blaming Ned for the drunk-driving accident. As she contemplated her father's steady, dependable payment of the loathsome "conscience money," she knew he had done his best to make it up to Josh for the injury he'd caused. He'd never missed a month, even to the point of going without medical care and other necessities for himself. He'd managed to keep his job and had stopped drinking—in short, he had made a genuine effort to change. It was even beginning to look as if, when he recognized the damage he'd done to Josh, he had wanted to atone for all the mistakes he made with his wife and daughter, too. That must have been why he'd straightened up his act....

"Aunt Lily Ann?" Sarah said worriedly, tapping her arm. "What's wrong? Why are you crying?"

Lily Ann stood at the living-room window, staring out at the rain drizzling down the pane. She hadn't even been aware of the tears streaking her cheeks as she thought about the countless times she'd judged her father with a standard of perfection he had never come close to attaining. He'd been human, and weak...an alcoholic, admittedly. But he'd loved her and her mother more than anything. Recalling the broken strand of pearls and the blue ribbon he'd saved all those years, she suddenly had to bawl. She wanted to see Ned just once more, to tell him face-to-face that she loved him and forgave him. But then, maybe he already knew that.

She wiped away the tears with her fingertips, then turned to find Josh standing behind Sarah, his expression even more concerned than his niece's.

"It's raining," Lily Ann said. "Rain makes me sad."

"It shouldn't," Sarah said in her most grown-up voice. "Don't you know what comes after the rain?"

"I'm always afraid the rain will never stop," she quipped, sniffling.

"You don't have to worry, Lily Ann." Sarah patted her hand. "The rain *always* stops. God promised never to drowned all the people again, no matter how bad we get. After it rains, God draws a rainbow in the sky to show He keeps His promises. It's a sign He loves us."

Lily Ann managed a smile. "I'll try to remember that from now on, Sarah."

"But it won't do any good to look for a rainbow when somebody else makes a promise. Like when you promised not to leave, I checked the sky." The little girl shook her head. "No rainbow. It only works for God. I asked Uncle Josh. He said with people, we just have to believe them or not believe them, because we don't get signs."

Lily Ann looked up quickly at Josh and saw a shadow of trouble, or maybe it was sadness, crossing his face. "Sarah, go find your brother," he said quietly. "Make sure he's okay."

He waited until he heard the child leave the room, then held out his hand to Lily Ann. When she moved straight into his arms, he pressed his mouth to her still damp cheek and kissed her there. For a long moment he didn't speak, then he said, "Are you unhappy here, Lily Ann?"

"No!" she gasped in horror. Her arms clenched around his lean waist. "Oh, Josh, no! I've never, *ever* been happier."

He touched the tips of his fingers to her face, and she wondered what he read in her expression. His own look was somber. "Is it . . . bad memories that make you cry?"

"It's memories, yes." Her voice was very small, cautious.

"Anything you can tell me about?"

Her heart lurched at the thought. "Not yet," she said, almost inaudibly. Maybe one day she would feel sure enough of Josh's love to confide her secret, but she was still afraid, terribly afraid, that that day was far in the future. She might forgive Ned, but would Josh ever? There was still his book, Baxter's story . . .

"Shouldn't you get back to work writing?" she asked Josh after supper. She needed to find out just how far Baxter's hunger for revenge would take him.

"Soon. I have one more item of business to take care of before I can concentrate on anything besides reality."

An icy chill ran down her neck. "That sounds serious."

"It is." He chewed on his lip, then reached out and caught her hand where she was wiping the table clean. Putting aside the dishcloth, he pulled her to him. "Lily Ann, if you meant your promise to stay—if you really are happy here, then I think we should begin the proceedings to adopt Sarah and Samuel. What do you—"

She didn't give him a chance to finish, but stopped his question with a kiss. "Yes, Josh! I'm ready! What do we do first?"

Smiling at her eagerness, he cradled her against his chest and rubbed his cheek against the silky crown of her hair. "First we see a lawyer, then I guess we ought to talk to the children and find out if they like the idea."

Three days later both tasks had been accomplished. Josh's lawyer had referred them to a specialist in family law who had agreed to get the paperwork started at once.

And Sarah and Samuel had been overjoyed at the chance to belong officially to Josh and Lily Ann. "You would really be our daddy and mommy?" Sarah kept asking. "Truly?"

"Really and truly," Lily Ann said, hugging both of the kids and Josh at the same time. It was without a doubt the happiest moment of her life up to that point.

She even had enough happiness to spare a smile for Betty Ludlow when she answered the front door that afternoon and found the social worker standing there, as dour as ever.

"Come in, Mrs. Ludlow." She felt a surge of pity for the woman. After all, Mrs. Ludlow had never had a husband as wonderful as Josh or children of her own like Sarah and Samuel. If she had, she wouldn't have ended up so crabby. "I'm glad you're here. We have some news for you."

"Do you, indeed, Miss Jones?"

"Mrs. Delaney," Lily Ann corrected her softly, her mood charitable.

"Oh, yes. Mrs. Delaney. I heard about your wedding." The woman gave her a cynical once-over. "Well, that's fine. I'm sure you think you've pulled a fast one. But I have something to say to Mr. Delaney. In private, if you please."

Lily Ann shivered with foreboding. "I'm not sure—"

"It's okay, Lily Ann," Josh cut in smoothly from the doorway of the study. "Show Mrs. Ludlow in. I'll handle this."

Chapter Fourteen

The door to Josh's study remained closed for thirty harrowing minutes. Meanwhile, Lily Ann found jobs to do out in the hallway. Since she also had to keep an eye on dinner, which was in the oven, and check on the children, who were building another sand castle, she feared she might not hear if Josh called her.

As it turned out, he didn't call. While she was in the kitchen, Mrs. Ludlow departed without a word. Hearing the front door shut firmly behind the social worker, Lily Ann hurried to look in at Josh and found him sitting at the desk as if frozen there, his face a stony mask. He looked so pale, so distant and unfamiliar, she might not have recognized him as the man she'd married—the man she had come to love more than any other soul on earth—if she hadn't known for a fact it was he who was sitting there.

"Josh?" she asked with alarm. "What is it? What did Mrs. Ludlow say to you?"

He didn't answer; she wasn't even sure he heard her.

Moving swiftly to his side, she put her hand on his shoulder, but the gesture only caused him to draw back as if her touch disturbed him.

"Josh, what's that woman done now? Is she still threatening to take the children away?"

Gradually his face changed as awareness of time and place seemed to stir through him. The skin at the corners of his eyes and around his mouth stretched taut, and he shifted his position in the leather desk chair, squaring his shoulders as he steeled himself. He tipped back his head and lifted his gray eyes until, despite their rather pensive, unfocused quality, they were aimed at her. The rest of his expression contained anger, accusation and shock all mixed up together.

Before he said a word, she had a sudden premonition about what was coming, and it made her heart tumble over.

"How long did you think you could keep your secret?" he asked with an icy calm that belied the emotions at war on his face.

Her breath catching in her chest, she gasped for air. "I—I—" Unable to finish, she stumbled backward and sank onto the sofa, trembling and weak-kneed.

"You do know what secret I mean, don't you?" he continued flatly. "Your father's name." Shaking his head, he exhaled, a harsh sound. "Ned Jones...Lily Ann Jones. I never made the connection."

She couldn't say a word. Although her heart hammered madly and her stomach churned with nausea, she wasn't afraid of being sick. As a matter of fact, the frantic thought occurred to her that a sudden heart attack might provide a way out of a situation that she had hoped and prayed would never happen. Obviously that particular prayer had gone unanswered. Shaking all over and dying inside, she sat and gazed at Josh through a haze of burning tears.

Slowly he reached up and covered his eyes, massaged his temples with thumb and fingertips, then rubbed his hand down his face. His marriage was a complete sham, and he hadn't had a clue. What a fool!

He hadn't wanted to believe Mrs. Ludlow when she first revealed the fruits of her investigation. He'd told himself it couldn't be true. Lily Ann wouldn't have lied to him— not his wife, his good friend and partner. Not his second half who went to sleep cradled in his arms every night, making him feel whole. Not his own personal warm-skinned angel who was fragrant and softly pliant, responsive to his touch, full of whispered love words. She couldn't have lied about something like this . . . about Ned Jones being her father. Ned Jones!

Something inside him twisted with the savage pain of being forced to remember the one person he'd worked hard to forget. After he was injured—after he realized what Jones's self-indulgent drinking had cost him—he hadn't wanted to hear that name ever again. He had been enormously relieved when the defendant pleaded guilty, because that spared him the ordeal of testifying at the trial. It would have been torture to be in the same room with the man who'd blinded him.

Months after it happened, Jeff told him about the day soon after the accident when Ned Jones had come to the hospital. He had stood alone in the doorway, gaunt and unshaven and hollow-eyed, staring with a look of mute misery at Josh's bandaged head as Jeff stared warily back at him from Josh's bedside. Then, with tears running down the deep grooves in his cheeks, the older man had turned to stumble away and had never attempted to meet Josh again. It was only a matter of weeks after the silent hospital visit, and after Josh had been released and gone home to the farm, that the money orders began to arrive every month. They started coming even before the court handed down its sentence, a sentence that didn't require any financial restitution.

The first time Jeff found a money order from Ned Jones in the mailbox, Josh ordered him to get rid of it.

His brother believed in making Josh do for himself, and that included making him think. "Any suggestions?" Jeff asked.

"Burn it," Josh snapped, not really caring what he did.

That had been too much for the practical, thrifty Jeff. "I'm not going to burn it. If you don't want it, I'm sure you can come up with someone who could use an extra hundred."

When Josh shrugged a refusal to exert his mental energy on such an exercise, Jeff stuck the money order into a desk drawer. "Whenever you decide where you want me to send it, let me know."

Josh had obstinately not given it another thought until a month later when a second envelope arrived from Wichita, Kansas, and Jeff got on his case again. To shut him up, Josh finally had him turn the money over to Reverend Oliver with instructions to use it to benefit the poor. He was glad to have the question settled because the money kept coming, never in huge amounts but with clocklike regularity, until about eight months ago. He hadn't known why the money orders stopped—hadn't *wanted* to know— until today when the social worker informed him that she'd found out Ned Jones had died some months back.

"Are you aware of the truth about Lily Ann Jones? Do you have any idea who you hired to look after your niece and nephew?" Mrs. Ludlow's words battered away inside his head, making him flinch again as he recalled them.

"Did you know you married the daughter of the man responsible for your blindness?"

While he was still reeling from that blow, she had pressed on. *"Now I ask you, Mr. Delaney—why would she come here if not because she hoped to take advantage of a blind man who also happens to have a lot of money? Why would she lie when I asked about her family background, if she didn't have something to hide? Obviously she didn't know I would be running a check on her through the state law enforcement computers, or she would have done a better job of keeping her stories straight. When I found that none of the information she gave me matched with the computer's data, naturally I began to look more deeply into her past and found out that her father was Ned Jones... the same Ned Jones convicted of driving under the influence and causing your accident. Did you know that when you hired her? When you asked her to be your wife?"*

No, of course he hadn't known. Instinct had told him Lily Ann didn't really have a lifelong desire to be a housekeeper—that she had taken the job through some quirk of reasoning that made sense only to her. But he'd never suspected her true motive for coming to his house that first night...whatever her true motive was. Just now, he wasn't up to speculating about it.

"Josh, I . . . I'm sorry I didn't tell you before today who my father was," Lily Ann finally managed. "I'm so sorry! But you've got to understand—"

While his enraged mind roared, *No more lies!* he interrupted her. "Be quiet, Lily Ann! Just—be quiet!" He gripped the arms of his chair and started to get to his feet, then clenched his jaw and sat down again. "I'd like to be alone," he said in a tired voice. Then, as it occurred to him, he muttered, "Do I dare trust you to watch Sarah and Samuel?"

She wrapped her arms around her waist and held on tightly as if to protect herself from his insinuations. "I'd never do anything to hurt those children, Josh."

He asked himself what he expected her to do—admit to being a child abuser? Knowing he had no choice but to trust her with the kids—and feeling like a bigger fool than ever because he trusted her in spite of everything—he nodded shortly and dismissed her. "Please leave me alone."

He heard her stand up and move to the door, then pause. "It's almost supper time," she informed him with all the dignity she could summon.

"I'm not hungry."

Still she waited. "Josh...*please*..."

He said nothing, his face rigid. Finally realizing the futility of trying to talk to him before he'd gotten over his initial wrath, she swallowed, blinked until she could see clearly again, and left Josh alone.

He didn't come out of his office all evening. Lily Ann fed the children at the usual time, putting on a good face for them as if nothing were the matter. They wanted to know why Josh couldn't eat with them and seemed pacified when she said he was working too hard to be disturbed. Tucking them into bed, she read them each a story. Since they hadn't had naps that day, they went right to sleep. That left her free to mope around while keeping watch over the closed door that separated Josh from the rest of the household.

The telephone rang around ten o'clock, and when Lily Ann picked up the receiver in the kitchen, she heard a male voice that she didn't recognize speaking to Josh. She hung up at once, not bothering to try to figure out who had called. Whoever it was, she somehow didn't think the call would help the mess she'd gotten herself into.

With each passing hour, her spirits sank lower as it became apparent that Josh wasn't going to talk to her tonight. Obviously he didn't want to hear her plead her case.

Maybe it was just as well, she thought as she slumped on the living-room sofa at 1:00 a.m. What could she possibly say to justify not having been honest with him about who she really was? How could she explain the horror that had gripped her heart when she'd finally realized what her father had done to Josh? Would he believe she hadn't known the truth when she first came to Bartlesville? That she hadn't learned the facts until she'd already fallen so far in love she couldn't think straight? She'd been scared to death he would hate her if he knew about her connection to Ned, and the way things looked, her worst fear was coming true.

Burying her head in her arms, she let her tears soak into the sofa cushion beneath her cheek. No excuse she could formulate would change the fact that she'd kept a secret from Josh...the terrible secret that her father had cost Josh his sight. It was her father who'd created Josh's obsession with revenge. Josh was never going to forgive her for being Ned's daughter and for not admitting it to him at the very beginning....

She fell asleep with her face pressed to the damp cushions and awoke to the sound of a door opening. When she sat up and rubbed her sleep-gritty eyes, she discovered that early morning light from the wall of windows had already brightened the living room. She must've spent the entire night on the sofa—for the second time since coming here, she realized ruefully.

Now that it was morning, maybe Josh would be ready to talk. That hope brought Lily Ann to her feet in spite of her cramped, aching muscles, and she rushed out into the hall.

Josh was about to walk out the front door, his folded cane in one hand. The fact that he'd just showered and shaved didn't disguise his lack of sleep or erase the shadows surrounding his eyes.

He made her think of a wounded warrior holding himself tall and proud as he limped off the battlefield, doing his best to hide the severity of his wounds from the enemy. She was the enemy! She had hurt him, had destroyed the trust he'd had in her.

Lily Ann watched him step across the threshold, her hope withering until she could stand it no more. "Josh!" she cried out. "Where are you going?"

He stopped and turned, his expression hard. "I don't know."

Peering past Josh, Lily Ann saw a brown-haired man waiting on the porch outside. This one looked like a professional football player—about the same height as Josh but having a much heavier build, with bulging muscles readily apparent in his short-sleeved shirt and tight jeans. His craggy face hinted at eons of experience, and he regarded Lily Ann with the vigilance of a hawk. His dark eyes were guarded, his stance alert as he stood there balancing his weight on the balls of his feet.

Shivering, she looked back at Josh. "How long will you be gone?" The plea in her voice echoed the desperation of her soul.

"As long as it takes." He seemed about to leave it at that but then gritted his teeth. "I can't tell you when I'll be back, Lily Ann. I just know I have to get out of here. There's something I need to do." With an impatient sigh he added, "Tell Sarah and Samuel I said goodbye."

The next moment he really was gone. Even after the brown-haired man pulled the door shut behind Josh, Lily Ann moved to the window and pushed aside the curtain so she could still see the two of them, crossing the porch and going down the steps together, Josh's hand resting on his companion's arm for guidance. The other man was saying something to Josh, at this point looking more worried than menacing. Josh just shook his head, his face bleak, and climbed into the black-and-tan Bronco that waited at the end of the sidewalk.

Lily Ann wondered if Josh's accident had felt anything like this to him—like the snuffing out of a light... the sudden extinguishing of the joy of living... a dark suffocating heaviness that seemed to smother the entire world...

Moving like a robot she made it through the day, her thoughts restricted to the task of trying to be cheerful for the sake of the children. Every sharp ring of the telephone, every car that slowed down as it passed by on the highway, every creak of the floor that sounded like a footstep, made her pulse jump with anticipation. Maybe it was Josh!

But it never was, and the disappointment became harder to bear each time she let herself hope. That first night, alone in the bed they'd been sharing since the wedding, she lay without even closing her eyes. In case he'd forgotten his key, she wanted to be sure she heard him arrive home so she could get up to open the door. Minute by endless minute, the night ticked away, and Josh didn't come.

Face facts, she ordered herself. He wasn't going to come home... not in the sense of walking through the door and gathering her in his arms to tell her how miserable he'd been while he was away from her. No, Josh despised her and everything she represented, and hating her, he couldn't possibly want to stay married to her.

By the next morning she found herself reverting to old habits and trying to keep her feelings on hold, because to do otherwise would have meant risking emotional collapse. If she looked beyond today and imagined a future without Josh, she really might flip out, and with the kids depending on her completely, this wasn't a very good time for that. The trouble was, old habits no longer worked very well for her. She still hurt no matter how hard she tried not to feel.

"But I don't understand, Aunt Lily Ann!" Sarah complained as she got ready for bed after her evening bath the second night without Josh. "Where *is* he? I need him to kiss me good-night."

"Don't we all!" Lily Ann blurted out the first response that came to mind, then gave her head an exasperated shake and brushed a hand over her eyes. She thought about Samuel, who'd quietly cried himself to sleep on his bedroom floor, in the midst of his menagerie of stuffed animals, after having trailed her around all day begging her to let him see his uncle. He couldn't seem to grasp the fact that she didn't have any control over the situation.

"Sarah, honey, I know you and Sam miss him," she said, kneeling to button the little girl's pajama top. "All I can do is promise you Uncle Josh will come home just as soon as he can." At least she'd been praying very hard that he would! "When he does get home, I'm sure he'll kiss you a dozen times to make up for tonight."

Sarah climbed into bed and reached up for a hug. "But I want him *now*," she said mournfully.

"Me, too." She held on to the child longer than usual, her throat hurting as she reflected that her chances of getting what she wanted were slim to none.

Lily Ann soaked for a long time in a hot tub, then slipped into Josh's bathrobe and curled up in his leather chair in the study. The robe was knee-length and belted, made of white terry cloth. Josh always looked incredibly sexy in it, especially when his black hair was tousled and wet from a shower, his eyes smoky with desire. Wrapping herself in the robe's soft thickness seemed to bring him closer. His scent, left over from the last time he wore it, filled her nostrils, so that when she shut her eyes, she could pretend he was here in the room with her. . . .

Forty-eight hours of nonstop worrying finally caught up to her, and her tired head drooped to one side. Lily Ann had just about dozed off when the sound of a car on the driveway snapped her back to wide-eyed attention. A moment later she heard footsteps on the front porch and the sound of a key in the lock. Her heart racing, she put her bare feet to the floor, stood up straight and stiff with apprehension, then slowly forced herself to walk out into the hallway to face the music.

Chapter Fifteen

Josh shut the door and then stood still for a moment, his shoulder braced against the door frame, his eyes so nearly closed that it seemed he could barely keep them open. Lines of fatigue etched his face, emphasizing every one of his thirty-four years. One glance and it was apparent that he'd gotten very little sleep while he was away from home. He was wearing the same khaki slacks and navy blue polo shirt, now fairly wrinkled, that he'd had on yesterday when he left, and his dark rumpled hair looked as if the only thing to comb it lately had been his fingers.

Lily Ann had never been more relieved to see anyone in her life. In her eyes, Josh couldn't look any handsomer than he looked right now—lines, wrinkled clothes, tousled hair and all. She wanted to throw her arms around him and beg him never to spend another night away from her.

Instead she stood silent and apprehensive and watched him prop his cane in the corner near the door where he sometimes left it, then straighten up slowly. She could see

the effort it cost him to gather his strength and inner will
and make himself move forward. He took two steps in her
direction and stopped, his expression undergoing a subtle
tightening as his senses alerted him to her presence.

Lifting his head, he seemed to look right at her, and she
saw a glint of steely determination cut like a laser beam
through the smoke-gray depths of his eyes. That formi-
dably purposeful look made her quake, because it told her
Josh had done some heavy thinking and had reached some
pretty serious conclusions. He'd made up his mind about
his marriage—and about his wife—without ever having
heard her side of the story.

Divorce. Lily Ann was almost certain that was what he'd
decided, yet she hoped she was wrong. Knowing of no argument she could make in her own defense, she tried not
to hope, because hope shattered would bring shattering
pain.

A moment later Josh moved forward again to approach her with bold strides, his jaw set in a display of
clear male stubbornness. Just before he would have run
into her if his radar hadn't been so keenly developed, he
halted and reached out, not giving her a chance to rally, to
move out of his way. When his fingers encountered her
chest and fumbled against the overlapped opening of the
soft robe, he let his eyes flutter shut for an unguarded instant and then when he'd opened them again, slipped a
strong arm around her. Clamping his hand over her
shoulder, he turned her around and headed down the hall.

"We've got to talk," he muttered hoarsely as he steered
her on an unerring path to the bedroom.

While Lily Ann's thoughts raced in circles, her heart had
slowed to a cadence of dread. *Please*, she prayed silently,
it can't be over!

Despite her fervent prayer, she figured he was about to tell her to pack up and get out. She might as well resign herself to the idea. It was what she deserved, anyway....

Once inside the master bedroom, Josh congratulated himself on remembering to switch on the light. He closed the door behind them and led her across the plush gray carpet to the bed. Pressing both hands on her shoulders, he sat her down on the quilted comforter before stepping back in a challenging stance. "I have to know why you did it, Lily Ann. Why did you lie to me?"

A long sigh quivered through her as she stared up at him. Her heavy aching heart acknowledged that he had every right to the truth. As much as it might hurt, as hard as it might be, she was going to bare her soul to him now.

"I just...didn't want you to hate me," she confessed in a voice so soft, so ragged, he had to tilt his head forward and strain to hear.

"I was afraid you'd hate me if you knew Ned Jones was my father. He hurt you so badly!"

Lily Ann had expected certain things to happen in this confrontation, but she had never anticipated what happened next.

Josh's expression softened and, as if painful regrets were marching past a reviewing stand in his mind, he caught his lower lip between his teeth. Moving to sit down beside her, he stretched out his long legs, then wrapped his arm around her again. This time, though, it seemed to be a gesture of sympathy rather than a way to keep her from escaping. "You're right—he hurt me. But your father's alcoholism left emotional scars on you, too, Lily Ann. I could tell something had made you afraid of love. I just didn't realize what it was, until I went to Wichita and talked to your friend Homer."

It was a good thing she was sitting, because her legs could never have stood up under such a shock. "You talked to Homer?" she gasped. "But...how...who told you..."

Gazing sideways at Josh, she could see his grim smile as he answered. "Mrs. Ludlow provided me with all the names and addresses I needed."

"Mrs. Ludlow..." Lily Ann felt faint, confused by Josh's unyielding tone, uncertain of what all this meant in terms of their relationship. Did he hate her or not?

"Mrs. Ludlow," Josh repeated. "It seems her agency has access to a law enforcement computer network, which comes in handy when they're doing background checks in cases of suspected child abuse. In cases like this, too, I guess," he said with irony. "Anyway, after all the trouble she'd stirred up, Mrs. Ludlow decided helping me was the least she could do." All of a sudden he chuckled rather wickedly. "I think she was afraid I might tear her office apart if she didn't cooperate...and I might have." His amused look vanished. As if he'd just reminded himself of something unpleasant, he withdrew his arm and stood up abruptly. "When I left here, I had pretty much reached the end of my rope."

"I know, Josh, and I'm sorry."

He didn't seem to hear her but began to pace back and forth across the big room. "I knew I had to find out what makes you tick, but it was obvious you weren't going to give me any answers. Thank God Kael made it back to the States at the right time to help. He knows all the ins and outs of conducting an investigation—"

The man who took Josh away was his friend Kael? It must have been he who'd called the night before Josh left, too—probably to announce his return. Lily Ann was glad Kael had been there when Josh needed him—glad he would be here now for Josh, even if it sealed her fate. She hated to think of him and the kids being at the mercy of some hard-hearted social worker when she moved out....

"I discovered that Homer had quite a few questions of his own," Josh was saying as he paced. "For some reason, he seemed to have mistaken me for a blackmailer." He paused and turned her way wearing a dry look that held at least a touch of humor in it, accented by one mockingly arched eyebrow. "I had to talk fast to convince him I'm respectable, especially when he found out I'd persuaded you to marry me. I don't think I measure up to his idea of the husband you deserve."

Lily Ann blinked, not knowing what to think of Josh's gentle teasing. Had he really tried to reassure Homer that she hadn't made a mistake in marrying him? Why would he have bothered, if he'd planned to kick her out of his life as soon as he got back home?

His mood suddenly turning stone-cold sober, Josh raked a hand through his hair. "Your father's best friend supplied some vital pieces to the puzzle, Lily Ann. He painted a pretty graphic picture of your childhood... the trouble between your parents. The fear and grief and worries that no little girl should have to handle. Homer admires you a lot, by the way. So do your friends in Springfield."

"My friends in Springfield?" she echoed in growing astonishment. "You went back to talk to Kathleen and Dina?"

With a tight-lipped nod he pushed his hands into the pockets of his slacks and thrust back his shoulders, trying to ease an ache of prolonged tension that had settled in his neck. "I left here intending not to return until I understood the mystery of Lily Ann Jones. I'd had all I could stand of not knowing. How could I help my wife get over the past if I didn't have the slightest idea what had hurt her? And when Mrs. Ludlow uncovered a completely different identity from the person I'd believed you were, it hit me like a ton of bricks that I didn't know you at all. However, thanks to those three old friends of yours, I'm starting to see—'' He broke off and managed a rueful shrug at his own terminology.

Her mind was spinning from the knowledge of where Josh had gone and what he'd done in the past two days. The one aspect of the whole thing that left her almost speechless was the discovery that he had done it out of concern for her! She could have understood his wanting to hurt her, to get back at her for her deception, perhaps even to destroy her after the way Ned had destroyed Josh's former world. But it didn't sound as if that had been his motivation.

A moment later, as if to underscore her thoughts, he found his way to the bed and stood right in front of her, reaching out both hands. With a touch that was sweetly familiar by now, and as heart-tuggingly evocative as the first time he'd brailled her, he skimmed deft fingertips over her face, interpreting the expression around her eyes and mouth. "Lily Ann... you've been able to forgive your father, haven't you? I've sensed a change in you lately."

Her voice tremulous, she whispered, "I've forgiven him, but...can *you* forgive him, Josh?" Salty tears blinded her. "And can you ever forgive me for not telling you Ned Jones was my father?"

The question seemed to make him stop and consider. Withdrawing his hands he stepped back slowly and gestured at his eyes. "At first I hated him for this. There were times when I didn't think I wanted to go on."

She'd suspected he must have had days like that, but hearing him say it called up a sob from the very bottom of her soul. She swallowed the sound with difficulty and didn't interrupt.

"Then gradually I began to realize that life is still good. Different from what it used to be, but sweet, nevertheless. It's composed of a lot of little things, individual moments of joy that stand completely on their own. Moments that sparkle like diamonds on black velvet. The way the earth smells after a rain...getting an unexpected hug from Sarah or Samuel...having a character in my imagination come to life with his own story." One corner of his mouth quirked upward. "Lately there've been a couple of bigger moments, too. I mean...really big ones! I've come to appreciate that life still holds the promise of excitement—that it's no less thrilling because I can't see it. As a matter of fact, it's the best kind of excitement there is—the kind that fulfills rather than leaving you always empty and needing more. So to answer your first question, yes, I've forgiven your father."

She wanted to believe him. Oh, how she wanted to believe what he said was true! But...

"But, Josh," she protested quietly. "The book you're writing...it's all about revenge!"

Surprise flitted over his features, then he smiled a little. "Not quite, Lily Ann. When it's finished, you'll find that this book is about the *absurdity* of revenge. How some people destroy their own lives, their last hope for happiness, by trying to get even with others."

All of a sudden it made beautiful sense to her. No, of course poor Baxter wouldn't have a happy-ever-after ending! Josh grasped that truth perfectly.

Relief filled her up like helium in a balloon, and she jumped to her feet, half expecting to float right to the ceiling. Before she could throw her arms around Josh, he was frowning, shaking his head, stalking toward the window, then turning to fling out an arm impatiently. "But I wasn't asking why you didn't tell me you were Ned Jones's daughter, Lily Ann. The answer to that is pretty obvious. Anyway, that's not the deception that really bothers me."

She regarded him with anxious eyes. "What makes you think I've told you any other lies?"

He inhaled shortly, then moved sideways with caution until his leg bumped the easy chair beneath the window. Preoccupied, he ran one hand along the overstuffed arm and heaved a deep sigh. Sinking onto the cushioned seat, he reminded her in a low voice, "You told me you loved me."

She studied his lean, dark face and his downcast air, searching for a clue as to what was bothering him. "Yes . . . so?"

"*So?*" He lifted his chin. "You made me *believe* you, when the real reason you married me must have been to atone for your father's mistakes." A tiny muscle hammered away in his cheek. "Don't you see anything dishonest about that?"

Was *that* what he'd been thinking? Her heart pounding with alarm and dismay, she dropped to her knees in front of him, then reached up to curve her palm against his rigid jaw. "Josh, you're wrong if you think I married you out of guilt! You're so wrong!"

"Why, then?" he demanded flatly.

"Why do you think?"

"To help me keep the kids." He shrugged. "Or because you felt sorry for me."

As she continued to caress his face, she felt a tender smile tug at her lips. "You don't believe that. You can't possibly!"

Watching him closely, she could see him thinking. He shifted his head a fraction of an inch so her thumb was touching the corner of his mouth. His lips parted and he swallowed, blinking as if the smooth warmth of her hand against his cheek dazed him.

"You tell me," he finally managed in a husky undertone. "Why did you marry me?"

"Because I love you!" Still on her knees, she stretched toward him and raised her other hand, too, weaving her fingers into his thick curls and smoothing the satiny hair back. She leaned closer and brushed a kiss across his sexy, beautifully shaped mouth. "I never lied to you about that, Josh. Besides, it would take a fool or a martyr to marry a man out of pity. *I* certainly wouldn't do it."

His hands reached out and grasped her slim waist to hold her in place while he thought about her words. "But the kids, Lily Ann...I know how much they mean to you. By the way, I'm sure it'll relieve your mind to know Mrs. Ludlow is no longer going to try to take them away. Kael took me to see Judge Robbins, and he assured me the adoption will go forward without a hitch."

"I'm glad, Josh, because you're right—they *do* mean a great deal to me," she said gravely. "It would have just about killed me if you'd lost the children. But much as I love Sarah and Samuel, I didn't marry you because of them. I'd already fallen in love with you a long time before you suggested that we get married to give the children a home."

"You had?" Josh was listening in that intent way of his. His breathing seemed to be suspended as he waited for her answer, not moving, assessing her sincerity with all of his focused energy.

"I had." Joyous love for him swelled up inside her until she wondered if she could contain it all. Keeping the children in their home, while certainly important, had merely been the excuse he'd used to marry her. She remembered now that on their honeymoon he'd confessed how his love for her was born the very first time he touched her.

"Oh, Josh!" She slid her arms around his neck and hugged him, glorying in his warmth, his appealing scent. "I promise you, I began to fall in love with you the first time I laid eyes on you."

Lean, hard hands tightened on her waist. Strong arms lifted her up off the floor and then pulled her down onto his lap. "You and your promises," he muttered, gathering her fragrant, supple, unbelievably dear length to him and enfolding her in an embrace that felt as if he never planned to let go.

She rested her head on his shoulder and ran her fingers through the soft thick hair on the back of his neck. "You'd better believe me and my promises, Josh! You opened the door to me that first night, and I was a goner. I'd never seen anybody so perfect, so magnificently *male*, and it scared the life out of me. I knew I should hit the road running just as fast as I could."

Josh didn't even want to think about how empty his life would be tonight if she had followed that first impulse, but he couldn't resist asking, "Why didn't you run?"

With her newfound freedom to be honest with him, she told him the truth. "Because I wanted to keep looking at you forever. Because I think my heart must have realized even then that you were going to be the best thing that ever happened to me." She nuzzled his ear. "And you have been."

Delicious tongues of fire began to lick along his nerve endings as a shudder of pleasure uncurled from the pit of his stomach. Somewhat distracted, he thought of how she'd rescued his family and helped restore his career, and how she was, even now, giving vibrant life back to his weary body just by lacing her fingers in his hair and planting kisses on his ear.

"*I've* been good for *you?*" he asked thickly, wryly.

"Mmm...you sure have! You're teaching me how to love."

In his heart Josh thanked God that Lily Ann had been so generously blessed with an abundance of love for others and that she was willing to share it with him. Privately he acknowledged that while he might have coaxed the love out of hiding, the capacity had been there all along. She'd just needed a little help tearing down the walls lonely experience had built around her heart when she was a child.

But he wasn't stupid. If she wanted to believe he'd taught her to love, well, what the heck? What harm would it do?

He loosened his hold on Lily Ann, gave her a gentle nudge off his lap and felt her get to her feet. A moment later he stood and promptly scooped her up into his arms again. Proceeding carefully across the room with his precious burden, he stopped when he reached the bed and bent down to place her in the middle of it.

Still leaning over her, he let his hands explore the silken mass of hair that spilled across the pillow. At the same time a picture formed in his mind of the blond, blue-eyed angel everyone had described to him...the shapely, lissome beauty his fingers had come to recognize and adore.

A smile of anticipation and immense happiness began to play around the corners of his mouth. He tried to hide it by lowering his head until his mouth hovered just above hers and announcing in a stern voice, "I think it's time for another lesson."

Lily Ann couldn't be fooled. She knew exactly how happy he was. Her own cup bubbling over with exultant

joy, she reached up to draw Josh down to her. "Yes, sir
Mr. Delaney, sir. Anything you say, sir!"

Giving in to the persistent pull of her hands, Josh set
tled his muscular length atop hers. "With that kind of at
titude, I'll bet you're the teacher's pet."

"Do you think so?" she asked with studied innocence,
wriggling and sending a flood of hot, fluid sensation
sweeping through Josh's middle.

"I know for a fact, the teacher's crazy about you," he
said, his voice hoarse with feeling. Enfolding her in his
arms, he kissed her throat. "I plan to make a career of
loving you, Mrs. Delaney." He added in a sheepish whis
per, "And that's one promise you can count on."

To the delight of the farmers around Bartlesville, an
unexpected summer rainstorm blew into northern Okla
homa just after midnight.

By sunrise, the showers had passed on to the east, leav
ing behind a countryside washed clean and a sky filled with
the biggest, the most vivid, the most providentially placed
rainbow Lily Ann had ever seen.

*   *   *   *   *

Take 4 bestselling love stories FREE

Plus get a FREE surprise gift!

Special Limited-time Offer

Mail to Silhouette Reader Service™

3010 Walden Avenue
P.O. Box 1867
Buffalo, N.Y. 14269-1867

YES! Please send me 4 free Silhouette Romance™ novels and my free surprise gift. Then send me 6 brand-new novels every month, which I will receive months before they appear in bookstores. Bill me at the low price of $1.99* each plus 25¢ delivery and applicable sales tax, if any.* That's the complete price and—compared to the cover prices of $2.75 each—quite a bargain! I understand that accepting the books and gift places me under no obligation ever to buy any books. I can always return a shipment and cancel at any time. Even if I never buy another book from Silhouette, the 4 free books and the surprise gift are mine to keep forever.

215 BPA AJH5

Name	(PLEASE PRINT)	
Address	Apt. No.	
City	State	Zip

This offer is limited to one order per household and not valid to present Silhouette Romance™ subscribers. *Terms and prices are subject to change without notice. Sales tax applicable in N.Y.

USROM-93R   ©1990 Harlequin Enterprises Limited

THIS SIDE OF HEAVEN

The miracle of love is waiting to be discovered in Duncan,
Oklahoma! Arlene James takes you there in her trilogy,
THIS SIDE OF HEAVEN. Look for Book Three in November:

A WIFE WORTH WAITING FOR

Bolton Charles was too close for comfort. Clarice Revere was
certainly grateful for the friendship he shared with her son.
And she couldn't deny the man was attractive. But Clarice
wasn't ready to trade her newfound freedom for love. Not yet.
Maybe never. Bolton's patience was as limitless as his love—
but could any man wait forever?

Available in November,
only from

R O M A N C E™

Silhouette Books has done it again!

Opening night in October has never been as exciting! Come watch as the curtain rises and romance flourishes when the stars of tomorrow make their debuts today!

Revel in Jodi O'Donnell's STILL SWEET ON HIM—
Silhouette Romance #969
...as Callie Farrell's renovation of the family homestead leads her straight into the arms of teenage crush Drew Barnett!

Tingle with Carol Devine's BEAUTY AND THE BEASTMASTER—
Silhouette Desire #816
...as legal eagle Amanda Tarkington is carried off by wrestler Bram Masterson!

Thrill to Elyn Day's A BED OF ROSES—
Silhouette Special Edition #846
...as Dana Whitaker's body and soul are healed by sexy physical therapist Michael Gordon!

Believe when Kylie Brant's McLAIN'S LAW —
Silhouette Intimate Moments #528
...takes you into detective Connor McLain's life as he falls for psychic—and suspect—Michele Easton!

Catch the classics of tomorrow—*premiering* today—
only from ✧ *Silhouette*